The Glass Cage

The Glass Cage

GEORGES SIMENON

Translated from the French by Antonia White

A Helen and Kurt Wolff Book

Harcourt Brace Jovanovich, Inc., New York

The Glass Cage

Chapter I

THE staccato sound of a typewriter woke him up, and he saw, as usual, the pale sheets of his wife's bed on the other side of the bedside table.

Who had decided there should be twin beds? After eighteen years, he could not say for certain. Moreover, the events of that period were blurred in his mind, and, for reasons that he did not try to analyze, he preferred to banish them from his memory. It was probably she. And he had not protested. He never did protest. In fact, they had never, even once, slept together in the same bed.

Even without the typewriter he would have awakened, for it was his time, seven in the morning, and one might have thought that it was at this hour every day that the noises in the street started up. This was not true. The life

3

outside had begun earlier, imperceptibly, but this was the moment when it suddenly broke through his sleep.

He remained torpid for a while, then got up, as if in a dream, and made his way dim-sightedly to the bathroom. He took a warm shower, for he had a horror of stretching out full length in the bath, in which he felt like a prisoner.

At that hour of day, such scraps of thought as passed through his mind were random and disconnected. When he shaved and saw himself close up in the mirror, he was not pleased with himself. His features were not clear-cut. They were weakly modeled, and his nose appeared to have no bridge. As for his dark eyes, they were large, protuberant, and expressionless. It was always his eyes that people looked at, and he suspected them of feeling a kind of uneasiness when they did.

He got dressed without taking the slightest pains to make himself look smart or attractive. He always wore dark suits, as if he wanted to be noticed as little as possible; yet there were always passers-by in the street who would turn and look back at him. He did not know why. It was a question he had asked himself ever since he was a child. He had the feeling of not being like other people, and when he was out he kept as close to the wall as possible.

Finally, he opened the door of the living room, where his wife was sitting at her typewriter, went over to her and brushed her forehead with his lips.

"Good morning, Jeanne."

"Good morning, Emile."

They must have kissed each other on the lips at one time, but that had not lasted long, and it had not left the slightest trace on their relationship.

In spite of the early hour, his wife was fully dressed. He had never seen her otherwise, for example, in a dressing gown or with her hair in curlers. She always got up before him. She left her bed noiselessly and shut herself up in the bathroom. Then she went into the kitchen to make the coffee. She ate two or three *croissants* that she found at the door, delivered along with the daily loaf of bread.

4

All this proceeded as regularly as clockwork, and he was so thoroughly accustomed to it that he saw nothing odd or abnormal in their behavior.

It was she who occasionally threw a brief glance at him as if to ascertain his state of mind that morning.

"I'll just finish my sentence; then I'll go and boil your eggs."

The boiled eggs of his childhood. At Etampes, where he was born and where his father was a baker and confectioner, his mother would go through the room behind the shop, then cross the yard, beyond which was the kitchen. He used to kiss his mother, too, on the forehead. His father, who had worked all night in the bakery, was already asleep upstairs.

His place was set on the oilcloth that covered the table. In those days he still put milk in his coffee. His mother had grey hair. She had turned grey very young, and this emphasized the freshness of her complexion, which later was to become blotchy.

She was still alive. They were both still alive and still carrying on their business.

He was a trifle embarrassed, now that he was forty-four, to be still eating two boiled eggs for breakfast. It seemed childish to him. His wife gazed at the alarm clock on the mantelpiece, and he slowly drank his first mouthfuls of coffee.

Neither of them spoke. They had nothing to say to each other. She wore a black skirt and a white blouse, with a cameo that had been given to her by her mother, pinned to the collar.

The furniture belonged to her, except for the twin beds they had bought together. She had been previously married for six months, and it was she and her first husband who had furnished the apartment. He worked as an accountant for a wholesale fabric firm on Rue du Sentier. He had caught pneumonia and died within a few days. His portrait hung on a wall of the living room. He had a fair mustache, and his hair was brushed up in a little tuft above his fore-

5

head. She had suggested removing the photograph, but he had said no. It did not bother him. He had even come to look at it with a fellow feeling.

He buttered his bread and ate it slowly, dipping it into the eggs. That, too, dated back to his childhood. Nearly always, the front doorbell had summoned his mother into the shop and he had been left to eat alone. He was used to it.

At school, he did not play in the playground. Nor did he chatter with the other boys. The teachers rarely asked him questions because his answers were invariably correct. He knew everything. What else had he to do but study when he returned home, at one end of the table in the kitchen, which was the center of the house, but where his father and mother made only brief appearances?

"Do go out for a little walk, Emile. You never take any air. You're quite pale."

His complexion was still pallid. He had never had any desire to walk in the streets or to look in shopwindows. Nor had he had any desire to play. The two bedrooms, his own and his parents', were above the shop. They were quite large, with low ceilings, and they were always dark, because the windows were not big enough. The bedrooms had no kind of heating. It was only in summer that he used to take refuge in his, with a book, and lie there, flat on the floor on his stomach.

Was there anything extraordinary about that? Why, then, did people always look at him with a kind of amazement and even his parents seem uneasy? Was it his fault that he found nothing to say to them? Both worked on their own. His father went down to the bakery to join Victor, the apprentice, at the hour when his mother went upstairs to bed after having closed the shutters of the shop. In the morning she got him his breakfast, after which he went straight up to bed.

It was perfectly satisfactory. Emile did not complain. Neither did he complain now.

"Do you mind if I go on with my work? They're coming for it at eleven, and I've still got two more pages to translate."

She was not good-looking, either. One could almost say she was ugly. She had very dark hair and a stout, rather stiff body. As for her face, it was what one calls a homely face.

He had always known this. He had never had any illusions about her looks. Perhaps it was because of her far from attractive appearance that he had become interested in her.

She was three years older than he. Even more. He was obliged to work it out; it seemed so long ago in the misty past. He had been two or three months over twenty-five when he had first known her, and she had been twenty-nine.

How had it all happened? It had taken months. They were both working for a printing firm—Jodet and Son's—on Rue du Saint-Gothard, opposite the railroad. Emile Virieu was a proofreader and worked in a glass cage on the ground floor, next to the press shop.

Jeanne's desk was in Monsieur Jodet's office on the second floor, which was reached by a spiral staircase.

Virieu often went upstairs to see his employer. For weeks he had scarcely noticed the young woman; then, little by little, he had grown accustomed to her.

He had to make up his mind someday. He could not live alone all his life. He occupied a room in the Hôtel des Carmes, near Place de la République, for he had formerly worked on Boulevard Saint-Martin. In those days he ate his meals in a little old-fashioned restaurant on Rue du Faubourg-Saint-Jacques, where he had his own table napkin in a pigeonhole.

Once a week he went to the movies. On the other days, he read. He had always read so much, since his childhood, that his head was stuffed with encyclopedic information.

One evening, when she left work at the same time as he did, he plucked up his courage and spoke to her.

"Would you care to come to the movies with me?"

She had stared at him in surprise, as if it had been the last thing she expected. She had stammered:

"I...I..."

Was she going to say she had an engagement that evening? He expected her to. He was resigned to it.

"I'd like to very much."

He had been so surprised that it had not occurred to him at once to thank her. The two of them had eaten at his little restaurant, but he had ordered extra dishes. She glanced at him surreptitiously.

"Do you live with your parents?" she asked him at last to break the silence.

"No. They're in Etampes, where they have a bakery and confectionery business."

"Haven't you any brothers or sisters in Paris?"

"I have only one sister, Geraldine. She's a year younger than me. She's married. She has three children and lives on Boulevard Diderot."

"Do you see her often?"

"No."

"Don't you get along with her?"

"Oh, yes. But they often go out in the evening. They have a lot of friends. On weekends they go off in their car to the country."

It cost him a great effort to answer these questions, and Jeanne could not think of any more to ask him, so that they ended the meal in silence.

Nevertheless, they were to meet again in the same restaurant. Their first dinner had taken place on a Thursday. As if by chance, their following meetings also took place on Thursday, which became their day.

At the printer's people watched them leaving together and joked about it. At that time, she was already living in the apartment where they lived now, and she was a widow. Was that why she wore black?

Now that they were both over forty, she still did so. She had no feminine vanity. She used no make-up except for a touch of powder.

"See you soon."

They lived on the second floor, and he went down the stairs slowly. He walked slowly, too, as if cautiously. There was a certain hesitation in all his movements.

And, as if out of humility, he averted his gaze from the passers-by in the street.

Rue du Faubourg-Saint-Jacques was swarming with people, its shops full of housewives doing their morning shopping. He edged in and out patiently and made his way to Rue Saint-Gothard, which was quieter, almost countrified. The printers were at work, and he waved vaguely to them as he walked toward his cage. It was against the wall, in the left-hand corner, and contained a long table facing the pressroom, a filing cabinet, and a smaller table.

It was May. He was not wearing an overcoat, only his black hat. For no particular reason, he had always worn a black hat.

He settled himself in his chair and glanced at the sets of proofs that had been put on his table.

The printing firm was not a very important one, and its presses were at least twenty years old. There were some twenty compositors and linotype operators, nearly all middle-aged.

Emile Virieu used a ball-point pen to make the conventional signs in the margin and write the words to be substituted. Being very good at grammar and spelling, he seldom needed to consult the dictionaries lined up in a row on his desk.

The time went by peacefully, for his work was no burden to him. Now and then he raised his head and looked at the pressroom beyond the glass partition. In his cage, he felt secure. No one paid any attention to him. They did not look at him as if he were a man unlike other men.

Was he? Ever since his school days he had wondered if he were. In any case, he did not feel the need to talk to them.

Nevertheless, one Thursday evening long ago, when they had left their little restaurant and he was escorting Jeanne back to her apartment, he had asked her:

"Have you ever considered getting married again?"

"I haven't thought of it up to now."

Pale though he always was, he had blushed.

"You haven't any reason for not doing so?"

"No. Of course, I've got my set ways. I'm no longer all that young."

"Neither am I. Do you know, for instance, that I still eat two boiled eggs for breakfast, just as I did when I was five years old?"

"That should be very good for your health. Who cooks them for you?"

"I do."

"In your hotel room?"

"Yes. One isn't allowed to cook there, but that can't be called cooking."

"No. Of course not. I suppose you have a hot plate?"

"That's right."

"I think I could easily get used to living with someone."

"Do you want to have children?"

"Not particularly."

"It seems I can't have them."

"That doesn't worry me."

"We'll talk about it again, shall we?"

He had waited for their next Thursday dinner without any feverish impatience. He was not in love. He remained calm, still with a slight fixity in his gaze. Was she, too, looking at him curiously, as if trying to understand him?

He could not remember what they had eaten that momentous Thursday. He was inclined to think it was little pork sausages cooked with spinach.

It was not he who had brought up the question he had asked her on the preceding Thursday. It was she who had said:

"Did you know I'm going to leave Jodet's?"

He had been completely dumfounded.

"Why?"

"Because it's work that doesn't interest me. My father

died when I was very young. My mother was a Russian ballet dancer. She decided to go off to America with an impresario who promised he could make her a success, and as I would have been in her way, she took me to England where she had a sister."

"Married?"

"Not then. She had a job with the B.B.C. I lived in London till I was nineteen. . . . I was a boarder in a school where I learned a great deal, and when my aunt did decide, late in life, to get married, I returned to Paris."

He listened without taking much in. Other people's lives did not interest him; neither did what they said. He had to make an effort to follow the conversation.

Was she going to give him a reason for not marrying him? If so, he wished she would say so at once. He gazed at her. He watched her lips moving. She was certainly no beauty, but that did not matter.

"I worked first in an office near the Champs-Elysées; then I came to Jodet's. Now I've decided to be on my own. With my knowledge of English, I'm competent to translate novels, which means that I could work at home. I went to see a publisher specializing in mysteries. I did a sample for him. He's satisfied with it, and he promises me as much work as I can manage."

"Are you pleased?"

"Yes."

"Then you don't want to marry me?"

"Why do you say that?"

"I don't know. It seemed to me. . . ."

"I had to put you in the picture. If you haven't changed your mind. . . ."

"I haven't changed my mind."

"In that case, there's nothing to stop our marrying. Have you considered that I'm older than you?"

"A little over three years. That makes no difference."

"I'm not very attractive to men."

"I'm not a male movie star."

"Have you had many mistresses?"

"No."

"Have you ever lived with a woman?"

"No."

"Have you got men friends?"

"No. I've never wanted to have any."

"Why?"

"I don't know. I don't feel at ease with people."

"You're a little shy, aren't you?"

"Perhaps."

"Do you go out in the evenings?"

"I go to the movies once a week."

"And the other evenings?"

"I read."

"So do I."

That was all he had done in the way of courtship. At the end of the month she had left Jodet and Son's and been replaced by a little blonde, much livelier. They kept on with their usual Thursday dinners.

There had been no church wedding. Neither of them were believers. They had got married at the town hall, and people whom they did not know had acted as witnesses.

Thus it was that Emile Virieu set foot for the first time in the apartment on Faubourg-Saint-Jacques. In the bedroom there were brand-new twin beds. The rest of the furniture dated back to Jeanne's first marriage.

Both of them had been embarrassed and awkward. They hesitated to get undressed, to make love. Emile had done so only rarely and always with prostitutes, and this had left him with unpleasant memories.

Each had gone in turn into the bathroom to get ready for bed.

"Which bed do you want?"

"I don't care."

"Then I'll take this one."

It was the one nearest the bathroom.

"I get up very early in the morning."

"I'm accustomed to getting up at seven."

"And what time do you go to bed?"

"Between ten and eleven."

"So do I."

They had both lain down in their own beds. She had switched off the bedside lamp. He had stayed motionless for a long time, his eyes staring into the darkness; then he had decided to get up and slip into her bed.

She had started but had let him do so. That time, he had kissed her on the mouth, without demanding more, and she had demanded no more either.

"So that's how you steal away my secretaries, Monsieur Virieu," Monsieur Jodet twitted him the next day.

He was a very thin, rather bent little man but, nevertheless, amazingly energetic. He had begun life as a compositor. He still quite often went down to the pressroom to give the printers a hand.

"She had already left you, Monsieur Jodet."

"I was joking. Besides, it's your own business, isn't it? Have you found an apartment?"

"She already had one."

"It's her second marriage, isn't it?"

"Yes. Her first husband had an untimely death."

"Happy?"

What could he reply? It was a word that was unfamiliar to him.

"I think I'm quite satisfied, yes. . . ."

Jeanne and he had spent four nights without being together again. At night, both of them lay down as a matter of course in their own beds. It was she who switched off the light, whispering:

"Good night, Emile."

"Good night, Jeanne."

He had to get used to calling her by her first name. It was easier in the morning, when he found her at her typewriter.

"You're sure you don't mind interrupting your work to boil my eggs?"

"No, of course not."

"I could easily boil them myself."

She cooked simply, without unnecessary elaborations. Her cooking was certainly as good as that in his little restaurant, yet he slightly regretted not going there. Here they were alone in the living room, which also served as a dining room. Each of them sat at one end of the big oval table, and they could hear the slow ticking of the pendulum clock in its carved walnut case.

He would have liked to have interesting things to tell her, but he could find only trite ones.

"Monsieur Jodet's son turned up in a new car."

"A sports car, of course."

"Yes. Everyone found an excuse to go and look at it."

The silence fell again. It did not seem to upset her. True, it had been like that ever since the beginning of their married life.

The day after their wedding, she had worked at her typewriter as usual. The three following nights, he had stayed in his own bed. It was only on the fourth night that she had come into his, without saying a word.

He had had a certain difficulty in making love. The first time he had tried, it had been with a prostitute of Rue Saint-Denis, and he had been twenty-two.

"So I've got to show you how to do it?" she had said, surprised by his inertia.

Little by little, life in the Rue du Faubourg-Saint-Jacques had acquired its slow, monotonous rhythm which was never to change in the course of the years. They went to the movies on Saturday evenings. They did not have a car. They could have afforded one, but who would have driven it? Emile Virieu would not have risked it, for he was often absent-minded. Jeanne did not suggest doing it.

They dined in town once a week, but not in the little restaurant where they had decided to get married.

They never quarreled. She continued to observe him

curiously, as everyone else did. In the evening, both had their armchairs and their books. Sometimes, if there was some good music, Jeanne turned on the radio.

Later, they bought a television set and, side by side, watched the programs.

It was a calm, dull life, yet this did not worry him. Only rarely did they visit his sister Geraldine, who had become Madame Lamark and now had three children. Her husband, Fernand, worked in the art department of an advertising agency on the Champs-Elysées.

It was noisy in their home. Everybody talked at once.

"I can't understand how, with your high-school diploma, you're satisfied with just being a proofreader. *I* didn't pass mine. Nor did I go to an art school. I haven't got any diplomas. Yet I've got an extremely good job."

What could he say to him? He was a tall, fair, elegant fellow who drank his two or three whiskies in the course of the evening. He talked in an authoritative way, as if he knew the answers to every problem. His sister had become a real Parisian.

They had a little house in the valley of Chevreuse and spent all their weekends there. In the winter they went off to the mountains for a ten-day skiing vacation.

To all the questions his brother-in-law asked him, Emile replied with a noncommittal gesture. He was not ambitious. Neither was he a rebel. He did not try to become anything other than what he was.

As for Jeanne, she did not push him. She could not have liked going to the Lamarks' in their brand-new, modern apartment on Boulevard Diderot any more than he did.

When, at the age of seventeen, Emile had returned from school and announced that he had got his diploma, his father had kissed him a little awkwardly on both cheeks while his mother wiped away a tear with the corner of her apron.

"Happy, sonny?"

He had replied, after thinking for a moment:

"I'm satisfied."

It was true. He felt a certain satisfaction because a part of his life was over and done with.

At home, everything smelled of tarts, confectionery, and new bread, warm from the oven. His father's apron was encrusted with flour.

"I hope you'll go on with your studies?"

"What studies?"

"Medicine, for example. I can just see you as a doctor. You look so serious and conscientious."

"I don't want to become a doctor."

"What about a lawyer?"

"Not that either."

"A professor?"

He would have been far too frightened of the stares of his pupils!

"I suppose you don't want to work with me and one day take over the business?"

"I must think it over."

He spent several days pacing the streets, turning over all kinds of thoughts in his large head. On Sunday, at table, he had announced:

"I'm going to try to learn your trade."

His father was touched and pleased. His mother was a little disappointed but consoled herself by thinking it would enable her to keep him at home.

He worked down below, in the bakery. He was not particularly awkward at the job, even though all his movements were slow.

"Shut the oven door again, son. . . . Hurry up. . . ."

This had lasted three weeks.

"I don't think I'd make a good pastry cook."

"That's up to you. You're free. What does appeal to you?"

"I think I'd like to live in Paris."

His father had given him a thousand francs. He had left on the bus. He had found a room with running water in a hotel on Avenue du Général-Leclerc.

He did not feel in any hurry. He did not try to discover his vocation, if he had one. Neither did he want to stay in Paris doing nothing at his parents' expense.

He read the small advertisements in the papers and presented himself at certain addresses. He was never the first to arrive. Sometimes there was a queue more than twenty yards long outside the door.

"Have you any references?"

"No."

"Have you never worked before?"

"I've just got my diploma."

People looked at him suspiciously, as though there was something inconsistent about him.

"We'll write to you."

They never did write to him, and the thousand-franc note had almost melted away. It was then that he had sold encyclopedias. He had a heavy single volume in his brief case. He started at one end of a street, worked down it to the other, then crossed over and worked all down the other side in the opposite direction. Most of the time, the doors opened only a few inches. A woman in a dressing gown surveyed him from head to foot.

"What do you want?"

He heard a child yelling. How could he hope to sell this woman an encyclopedia in twelve volumes?

"I would like to show you a book."

"I've no time for reading, and when my husband comes home, all he wants to do is listen to the radio."

He was not discouraged. In spite of everything, he sold two complete sets. One day he tried the Grands Boulevards, and, starting from the Place de la République, he walked up Boulevard Saint-Martin. The houses were old, some of them dilapidated.

On one door, an enamel plaque bore the words:

Samuel Bloomstein
Stamp Collections

And above the bell:

Enter without knocking

He entered. The walls were covered with rows of pigeon-holes, and a bald man with a magnifying glass in his hand was bent over some postage stamps.

"What can I do for you?"

A dead cigarette hung from his mouth. His eyebrows were thick and bushy. He looked up at Emile and frowned.

"What do you want to sell me?"

"The best of all encyclopedias."

He began to open his brief case, but Bloomstein stopped him with a gesture.

"No use. The best encyclopedia is the one I have here."

He tapped his forehead and gave a little chuckle.

"How old are you?"

"Eighteen and a half."

"And is this all you've found to do?"

"I've sold some."

"How many?"

"Two sets."

"In how long?"

"A month."

"When you were a boy, did you ever collect stamps? Nearly all of them do."

"No."

"Do you know a little geography?"

"I've got my diploma."

"Instead of going round knocking on doors, wouldn't you rather work with me?"

He was engaged the same day and started work the following morning. The room above the ground floor had a low ceiling, and when one opened the window to air the room, the roar of the traffic assaulted one's ears. The roofs of buses, which sometimes went past in double file, looked like the backs of huge elephants.

He had covered a little table with brown paper, secured

with thumbtacks. Bloomstein handed over to him job lots of stamps, several hundred at a time, and he had to classify them by countries. On one corner of the table he had a list of stamps that had to be kept apart from the others.

In summer it was very hot, in spite of the trees outside, which gave some shade. His other job was to fill up the cellophane envelopes. There were two-franc, five-franc, and ten-franc ones. It was easy. There were some beautiful stamps that up to then he had never known existed.

Bloomstein himself dealt with the rare stamps and received the collectors.

"I'm pleased with you, young man. I'm raising your salary fifty francs as of next month."

To see closely, Emile had to wear thick glasses, and when he went up before the Army Medical Board at Etampes, he was rejected for military service. He was not especially delighted. He might perhaps have liked being a soldier.

His sister, who was a year younger than he, was engaged at the time. She worked in Paris, in the same advertising agency as Lamark on the Champs-Elysées.

He had to go to the wedding. The Lamark relatives were there, and various friends. Everyone dined at the Cloche d'Or, and in the evening his father was more boisterous than usual.

"What about you? Aren't *you* going to get married? Still at your old stamps?"

He laughed. That night everything seemed to amuse him, whereas Emile kept himself aloof as much as possible.

No, he was not ambitious. He had his room, two steps away, on Place de la République. The hotel was clean, the room almost spacious, and there was a bathroom at the end of the hall. Why the hotel was called Hôtel des Carmes—Carmelites—he had never asked, and no doubt the manager had no more idea why than he had.

It is true that the restaurant on Place des Vosges where he took his meals was called, equally oddly, "Chez d'Artagnan." He always sat at the same table, not near the window, but at the back where the light was rather dim.

Though he did not deliberately conceal himself, he did not like being stared at.

He stayed more than four years with Bloomstein. Once, he spent his vacation making a tour of France by train, stopping in all the big cities for two or three days.

"Are you taking a girl friend with you?" his father had asked him.

"No."

"Well, my boy, if I'd toured all around France at your age, I'd . . ."

"Don't boast, Gaston," his wife had interrupted sharply.

One evening he had read in the paper that there was an opening for a proofreader at a printer's on Rue du Saint-Gothard. He had asked for a day off to go for an interview. Monsieur Jodet had received him in his office on the second floor, the other occupant of which was an elderly lady who appeared to be his secretary.

"Are you a good speller?"

"Yes. I've got my diploma."

"What are you doing at the moment?"

"I'm working with a stamp dealer."

"What salary do you want?"

"I don't know."

Monsieur Jodet was thin, high-strung, and abounding with energy. He turned to the old lady, who Emile later learned was his sister.

"Shall we give him a trial?"

They printed mainly small editions of books, pamphlets, university theses, collections of poems at the authors' expense.

In the morning, when he installed himself in his glass cage, there was perhaps a momentary sparkle in his eyes. Was this not the dream of his life? He possessed a few square yards that were his exclusive domain, bounded by a glass partition that separated him from the presses and the workmen.

He saw the men going to and fro, consulting each other,

lighting a cigarette after making sure the boss did not see them.

They paid no attention to him. For them, he did not exist. He worked slowly, with scrupulous care. Often he came across impossible sentences and took it upon himself to amend them.

Madame Françoise, as they called Monsieur Jodet's sister, was over sixty-five. They learned that she was going to retire to the country where she owned a small house, and one morning Jeanne arrived to take her place.

Emile paid no attention to her. It was she who stared at him, with a touch of surprise, as if he were different from other men. He went up to the office in the morning and afternoon to collect new sets of proofs or to take back the ones he had corrected.

Jodet's son, Jean-Jacques, theoretically occupied the adjoining office, but he was seldom there. He was twenty-five, and his contribution to the firm consisted in spending mostly on cars, the greater part of what his father earned by hard work.

There was a Madame Jodet, the wife of the father, who came to the office at long intervals, when she needed something. She must have been ten years younger than her husband. Emile took her to be about fifty, but he was no expert in such matters.

She was a buxom woman, pink and white as sugar icing, with a faint mauvish tint in her cheeks, and she always wore enormous necklaces. It would have been difficult to find two people more unlike each other than she and Jodet. She walked with her head held very high, and the workmen claimed that she forced him to go out nearly every evening.

Emile's life was calm. Once a month he paid a visit to Geraldine.

"Your work isn't too monotonous?"

"Why, no."

"At least you eat well."

"As well as one does in any restaurant."

"Why aren't you married yet?" his brother-in-law asked him. "What are you waiting for?"

"Till I want to."

"You might have children."

It was the year that Geraldine was pregnant for the second time. Emile did not react. Children had no sentimental appeal for him. He kept on going, accepting life as it was without asking himself questions. It was others who asked themselves questions about him: he knew it; he read it in their eyes and merely turned his head away.

Madame Jeanne, as they called her at Jodet's, had a plain, homely face. She obviously knew it. She resigned herself to it and used no artifice to correct its defects.

At heart, he was very fond of her. Fond was too strong a word. She inspired his confidence. If he had had a problem to submit to someone, he would have submitted it to her.

One year, two years had gone by since she had come to work in Monsieur Jodet's office. Had the idea of marrying her been at the back of Emile Virieu's mind all that time?

He was incapable of saying. He did not dream of passionate declarations or of passionate embraces. Neither was he sentimental. It seemed to him that he was incapable of saying to a woman:

"I love you."

Physically, he had few needs. At long intervals he went with a prostitute he picked up in the street. He was a little frightened of them, for, better than anyone else, they sensed at once there was something odd about him.

Sometimes he wanted to ask:

"What is peculiar about me?"

For he did not know, and sometimes it worried him. These women he went with were certainly curious about him but also seemed somewhat afraid of him.

They did not question him. They got through the business as quickly as possible, and when he left he walked with a heavier step.

Why should he not get married? If Madame Jeanne was not good-looking, if one could even say that she was ugly, so much the better. Could he aspire to marry a pretty girl? Would he not feel embarrassed, even humiliated, in her presence?

Not to mention the fact that pretty girls are vain and exacting, that they would make every effort to change his way of life and even his way of dressing.

He thought the matter over for months before inviting Madame Jeanne to have dinner with him in his little restaurant. He did not even know that she had been married before, and when he learned this he was rather pleased than otherwise.

Chapter II

THE first year, neither of them had talked of taking a vacation. Jeanne was working on a long American novel that was giving her trouble because it was full of slang words, and this obliged her to keep consulting a dictionary of slang.

Emile walked about the streets, seldom going beyond the Seine, where he browsed among the bookstalls on the quays.

He was not bored. He was never bored. He had no conception of what it meant. According to his mother, when he was a baby he could sit for hours in his high chair, staring into space. He did not cry. Neither did he smile.

"I was worried. You weren't like other babies, so I took you to Doctor Lovit for him to have a look at you. He asked me if you ate well and if all your functions were normal, and he told me not to fuss."

What disturbed him now was having his daily routine altered against his will. People would have found it incomprehensible that he should continue going to Rue du Saint-Gothard instead of taking the vacation to which he was entitled. And yet he missed his glass cage. It had become his lair, his refuge, just as the room at the stamp dealer's had been for several years.

He stared at people without seeing them. He was not interested in the passers-by, and it was perhaps because they sensed this that they turned their heads to look back at him.

Doctor Lovit had been their family doctor. He was very gentle, very calm, and he had a grey, almost white beard that was always well groomed. He was a widower and lived with a middle-aged housekeeper who watched over him like a dragon.

When a patient telephoned him in the evening, for example, or at mealtimes, she insisted on knowing what was the matter, and it was she who decided how serious the case was.

"I assure you the doctor can't go to see you before six."

Emile must have been about twelve when his mother once again took him to Doctor Lovit.

"I don't know what's the matter with him, Doctor. When he's ill, it's not easy to make him admit it."

"Come on, my little friend, tell me what's wrong."

"I've got a headache."

"Do you often have them?"

"Nearly every day."

"Very bad ones?"

"Perhaps. It gets me there."

He indicated the back of his skull.

"Have you been having them long?"

"Several weeks. Maybe several months."

"And when you have one, does it last long?"

"All day. Sometimes it wakes me up at night."

He examined his eyes.

"You're good about wearing your glasses for reading and writing?"

"Yes."

"Is your digestion all right?"

"I never have a stomach-ache. Except that when I get this pain in my head, I feel as if I'm going to be sick."

"And are you sick?"

"No."

"Do you have a bowel movement every day?"

"Yes."

He was annoyed with his mother for having brought him to see Doctor Lovit. He did not like being asked questions.

"Show me your tongue."

Then he had to lie down on the imitation-leather-covered table, and Lovit had prodded him all over.

"I can't find anything wrong. Have you taken aspirin?"

"I haven't taken anything."

"Try aspirin. Not more than three a day and only when the pain's very bad."

The aspirin had not had the slightest effect. The pains continued, more violent than ever, and though he took care not to complain, his mother guessed and took him once more to see Lovit. They had waited more than an hour in the waiting room, where there were five people ahead of them. Luckily, there was a young girl to serve in the shop when Madame Virieu was out.

"Well? No better?"

He examined him again. Pressing on his liver, he asked him:

"Am I hurting you?"

"No. You're tickling me."

"Do you worry a lot over your work at school?"

"No."

"Do you play with your friends?"

"No."

"Why not?"

"Because I haven't any friends, and I don't like playing."

"He's always buried in his books, Doctor."

"It's probably nerves. I'm going to prescribe a sedative for him."

Was it the effect of those pink pills? He had had no more headaches for several months. Since then, they had returned from time to time and lasted some days, occasionally two or three weeks. He no longer paid any attention to them. He did not like being examined, especially as each time the doctor looked at him with a kind of amazement.

His parents never took vacations. So they sent him and his sister to stay with an unmarried aunt who lived in Fouron, a village near the forest of Orléans.

"You need good air."

As if there were not good air in Etampes. At Aunt Lucille's, who spent her time scouring her floors and polishing her furniture, there were no books. For Emile, those vacations were torture.

"Why don't you go and play with your sister in the woods?"

"Because I don't want to."

The first vacation that he and Jeanne took together was spent at Les Sables-d'Olonne, where they stayed at the Hôtel Royal, on the embankment. From their windows they could see the vast flat beach, with a pine wood on the left and the jetty of the harbor on the right. Thousands of bathers were splashing about in the sun-splashed water, and one could see the white edge of the sea slowly advancing as the swimmers dashed into it. In the distance the fishing boats cruised to and fro tirelessly.

"Shall we go in for a swim?" he suggested.

"Yes, if you like."

They were given a cabin for two, a red canvas cabin surrounded by women lying stretched out full length sunbathing.

"Are you going first?"

"No. You."

He had pulled down the canvas flap and undressed with embarrassment. His body was dead white. Even as a child he had always been rather too plump, and now he was adipose, with rolls of fat around his waist. He very nearly got dressed again but dared not, because of Jeanne.

He emerged, carrying his bath towel.

"All yours."

She was no more enthusiastic than he was, and she stayed a long time in the canvas cabin. The one-piece bathing suit she had bought before leaving Paris was red. She had tried in vain to find a black one. At last she came out in it, ashamed of her appearance.

She had large, pendulous breasts, a protruding stomach, and varicose veins, which traced patterns on her calves and thighs like the rivers on a map.

They ran down to the sea. Neither of them could swim. They waded into the water, which was shallow at first but ended by coming up to their chests.

"You're not cold?"

It was a failure. They were both ashamed of themselves and felt humiliated by the children who were swimming all around them. They had never realized that they had such unhealthily pale skins.

People paid no attention to them. There were too many even to notice them. Thousands crowded the beach from one end to the other. When Virieu had passed through Les Sables during his tour of France, it had been in early spring, and the seaside resort had not yet been invaded by hordes of holiday makers.

They did not lie down and sun-bathe. They went straight back to their tent, and Jeanne asked him if she could go in first.

He did not like the crowd. The men frightened him. When it was his turn to get dressed, it was a relief to be back in his everyday clothes. They took to walking along the embankment instead of going down to the beach. Sometimes they went to the market, where the fish were laid on stone slabs and the fishwives wore sabots and short kilted skirts.

They felt awkward and out of place. They had decided, in Paris, that they would stay three weeks or a month. After a fortnight they returned home.

The following year, Jeanne had an urgent piece of work, the translation of the memoirs of an English statesman. It was Monsieur Jodet who recommended that Emile go to an inn on the banks of the Loire, between Nevers and Pougues-les-Eaux.

"Your wife will find it a very good place to work. There are never more than two or three families staying there."

It was true. Jeanne installed herself with her papers and dictionary on a terrace that was more like a pergola, a great tunnel of greenery. The sunshine filtered through the leaves and made quivering patches of light here and there on the paving.

Emile had brought some books. Nevertheless, he sometimes went for a walk by himself in the woods. A middle-aged couple walked six or seven miles every day and bathed in the Loire in the late afternoon. A man with a huge brown mustache went fishing all day and often returned with a net full of fish.

Virieu knew nothing about fishing. Nevertheless, he went to the neighboring village and brought a cheap fishing rod and some lines. He installed himself a few yards away from the fisherman, who looked at him with a slight frown.

The red float moved slowly over the sparkling water and occasionally bobbed and disappeared. Emile pulled in his line, but there was nothing on the end of it.

"The fish are cunning around here. Like the local inhabitants. Have a drop of white wine."

His neighbor drank it all through the day, and in the evening his face was purple. The cooking was good. Two couples had children who bathed in the river, which had an island of pebbles in the middle of it.

Jeanne's work was progressing well. In spite of the

noise, in spite of the hens pecking all around her, she managed to concentrate, and at the end of the first week she was able to send some twenty pages to the publisher in Paris.

Had Emile eaten something that disagreed with him? Or was it the local white wine? He had a severe attack of diarrhea, and, as it persisted, he decided to go and consult a doctor in Nevers.

His name was Brabant. He was quite young. He looked at his patient as if something in the latter's aspect surprised him. Was it his prominent eyes, devoid of all expression?

He asked him a few questions and palpated his stomach and diaphragm.

"Is there anything else wrong with you?"

"I sometimes have violent headaches that last for several days."

"Have you consulted a doctor?"

"Yes. He says it's due to nerves, and he's prescribed sedatives for me."

This surprised the young doctor, who began to feel his skull in various places.

"Is it here?"

"Yes."

"Do the sedatives work?"

"More or less."

"Have you suffered from these headaches for long?"

"Since I was a child."

"Have you got your medicine with you?"

Emile produced the little box of pink pills. The doctor examined them.

"I see."

He did not explain himself. He looked rather grave.

"Are you married?"

"Yes."

"Do you get on well with your wife?"

"Yes. We never quarrel."

"You haven't any worries in your professional life?"

"None."

He seated himself at his desk again and began to write out a prescription.

"You are to take one of these powders three times a day, diluting the powder in a little water. Not too cold water—preferably warm. That's for your bowels. As to your headaches, I'm not competent. Perhaps, when you return to Paris, you might consult a neurologist."

What was the use? No one understood anything about him, and he had ended by accepting himself as he was. He walked back through the woods to the inn, where Jeanne was still working on the terrace.

"What did he say?"

"He prescribed a powder for me that I'm to take three times a day in a little warm water."

He took the prescription to the pharmacist. The medicine was an ordinary one. He remembered having taken it when he was about thirteen and had had dysentery. There had been a storm that day. The weather remained unsettled for two or three days. The clouds hung low, and from time to time there was a long shower of transparent rain that fell straight down from the sky and bounced up from the ground as it touched it.

Jeanne worked in the public room of the inn, where the local peasants dropped in to drink their pint of white wine. Emile read. Between the showers he went for a walk, but he no longer attempted to fish.

He never wondered if he was happy. It was a word that, for him, had no meaning. He continued to live like a piece pushed from square to square on a chessboard, without asking himself questions.

They stayed at the inn till the date they had set themselves and returned to Paris, where their apartment smelled stuffy from having been shut up so long. Many of the shops on Rue du Faubourg-Saint-Jacques were closed, for it was not yet the end of August. In the morning they had to go and get the *croissants* and the loaf of bread from a bakery they did not ordinarily use. Only the butcher had returned from his vacation, with a rich sun tan.

Monsieur Jodet had returned, too, but his wife had stayed on at Juan-les-Pins, where she spent every evening in the casino.

Virieu and his wife had married under the legal arrangement of separate maintenance, according to which each party retained and administered his own property. This had seemed the natural thing to both of them.

At the end of each month Jeanne presented him with the account of what she had spent on food and housekeeping, and he paid her his half of it.

She no longer came into his bed. That had lasted only a few weeks, perhaps a couple of months. Neither did he go into hers. This did not worry either of them.

In the fourth or fifth year of their marriage they had bought a television set, and they spent most of their evenings watching the programs.

At the printer's Emile still felt as content as ever in his glass cage, which isolated him from the rest of the world. The workmen were so used to him that they were no longer surprised to see him sitting there for hours without moving. They left their posts for a few minutes, about ten in the morning, to go and have a glass of red wine in a nearby bistro. This was part of the ritual of the firm, and Monsieur Jodet had no objection to it.

"How's Jeanne?"

She had been his secretary long enough for him to call her by her Christian name.

"She's very well. They give her more translations than she can do."

"Do they pay her well?"

"I've no idea what they pay her. I've never asked her."

And Monsieur Jodet, like everyone else, looked at him with a surprised expression.

At the time when the printers went out for their drink, Jeanne left the house to do her shopping. The tradesmen all knew her. The butcher, especially the pork butcher, appreciated her ability to recognize first-class meat.

She was a good cook. She took as much pains when she was working at her gas stove as when she was working at her translations. She nearly always had the radio on when she was cooking, and that kept her company.

Emile returned from work a little after quarter past twelve. He went straight to the bathroom to wash his hands. They did not kiss each other. They did this only in the morning, and they still kissed each other on the cheek or forehead.

Could one say they were good friends? Perhaps. They felt at ease with each other and did not talk much, as if there were no need to.

She accompanied him when he went to see his sister, about once a month. They could not go on Saturdays or Sundays, because the Lamarks went to their country house on weekends.

Fernand Lamark must have been promoted, for they spent more and more, and they had a new car.

Emile did not envy them. He did not envy anyone.

It was years now since Jeanne had had any news of her mother. It is true that the latter had written very seldom since she went off to America. She was no longer a young woman. Had her impresario married her? Or was she eking out a living by giving dancing lessons and trying to get bit parts on television?

She had never bothered about her daughter, and Jeanne could hardly remember what she looked like.

"She was a beautiful woman, very attractive."

This was almost all that she could recollect of her.

"My aunt was quite different. You'd never have taken them for sisters."

Jeanne herself had had an uneventful life, and she had married Emile. Did she regret it? If so, she showed no sign of it, and he never saw her anything but relaxed.

"Are some of the tenants moving?"

He had just seen a large yellow moving van in front of the street door.

"It's our neighbors in the opposite apartment."

There were two apartments on the second floor facing the street, their own and the one that, up to the day before, had been occupied by an elderly couple.

They were such quiet people that they were hardly aware of their presence. They had married children. One of the daughters had gone to Australia with her husband and had several children. One of the sons, who was a lawyer, had his apartment and his office on Rue Gay-Lussac. They must have had another daughter, but she never came to Rue du Faubourg-Saint-Jacques. Perhaps she, too, lived abroad?

"Do you know where they're going to live?"

"They're leaving Paris. According to the concierge, they've bought a villa in Antibes."

The man must have been seventy-five, his wife five or six years younger. And now they had suddenly decided to change their whole way of life.

"They must be well off."

"They'll have the villa to leave to their children."

They themselves had no children. Each of them earned a comfortable living. When they were the same age as their neighbors, or even sooner, they could buy themselves a villa on the Côte d'Azur.

Emile had no desire to. Vacations had given him a foretaste of life in places besides Paris.

If, one day, he were to buy himself something very expensive, it would be an apartment like Monsieur Jodet's, overlooking the Seine. Monsieur Jodet lived on the Quai Bourbon on the Ile Saint-Louis and had a view of the two arms of the Seine and the cathedral of Notre Dame.

Not a large apartment. Luxury did not appeal to him. For himself, he would have been content, if necessary, with one room, as in the days when he lived near Place de la République.

. . .

One Saturday in June they decided in the morning to go and spend the afternoon at Etampes. They could not go there on a Sunday because that was the day when there was most demand for pastries and the shop was busiest.

They took the train at the Gare d'Austerlitz, and, when they reached the little town, it lay somnolent under a broiling sun and the heat was oppressive. It had often been like that in summer during his childhood. He remembered one year when the schools had been shut for days because of the heat. That, too, had been in June.

Once again he saw the almost deserted streets, cut in two, one half in the shade, the other in the blinding sunlight.

It gave him no pleasure to revisit his home town. He had no desire to see its familiar streets and sights again— for instance, the ice-cream seller with his gaudily colored cart adorned with a crudely painted view of Vesuvius and a panorama of Naples.

The man, of course, was not the same. Perhaps it was his son or someone who had bought the cart from him.

The one in the old days was called Angelino. He had had a magnificent grey, or rather silver, mane.

Emile conjured up his memories without a trace of nostalgic emotion. He mopped his brow, and, when he pushed open the door of the shop, automatically jingling the bell, it was as if he had never set foot in this house before.

A new, very young salesgirl stood behind the counter. His mother chose them young in order to pay them less, and the work was neither difficult nor tiring.

Beyond the room behind the shop, both doors of which were open, he saw his mother coming across the yard, wiping her hands on her apron.

"Emile! What a nice surprise."

She kissed him on both cheeks. He was not tall, but she was shorter than he and had to stand on tiptoe.

"And Jeanne, too. How are you?"

She kissed her, too.

"You weren't too hot walking here?"

He looked at her as he might have looked at any other object. She was, he knew, his mother. He came to see her several times a year without any contact being established between them.

She had aged a great deal and, above all, put on so much weight that she had some difficulty in moving. Her hair had grown very thin, and she coiled it in a meager bun at the nape of her neck.

"Come along, children. I'll go and make you a nice cup of coffee."

The room behind the shop had become a little parlor. There was a round table in the middle covered with one of those cloths sold by Moroccan peddlers and a vase of artificial roses. There were also two leather armchairs and a television set.

"Sit down here. It's cooler in here than anywhere else, because of the draft."

He had been born in this house. He had lived in it for eighteen years. Yet it was more unfamiliar to him than his glass cage on Rue du Saint-Gothard.

His father, in white trousers caked with flour and an undershirt that left his arms bare, came across the yard in turn.

He held out his hand somewhat awkwardly. He was not sure whether one shook hands with one's own son, and he was not in the habit of kissing him. He held out his hand to Jeanne, too.

Of the two, he had aged more. Instead of getting fat, like his wife, he had grown thinner. His cheeks sagged, and there were bags under his eyes and loose folds of skin on his neck.

"Do sit down, children,"

Each time Emile promised himself:

"I won't come again."

Then, mechanically, he would decide, one fine day, to go and pay another visit.

The walls were lined with shelves on which tarts and cakes were set out on wicker trays.

"What's the news of you both? Have you kept well?"

"Very well."

"I find myself getting tired these days. It's true I get through as much work as I did when I was twenty. I don't know how your mother manages. She's on the go all day, and in the evening she finds time to darn my socks."

"Why don't you both retire?"

"And how should I fill up the day if I retired, with nothing to do from morning to night? I bet that after the first month I'd get ill. Here, we live by the clock; there's always the bakery waiting, the tarts to be made, the customers to be served. I'm only seventy-four, and I'm good for a few more years yet, unless one of these days I drop dead like a horse that drops dead in its shafts. Are all of you drinking coffee? Wouldn't you rather have a glass of white wine? That's what keeps *me* going."

"Yet you know the doctor told you not to drink it."

"If one only did what the doctors let one. . . ."

He went into the kitchen to get himself some and returned with a glass in his hand. His wife took advantage of his absence to whisper:

"He's taken to drinking a lot. It worries me."

"What were you talking about?" he asked.

"I was going to tell them about Geraldine. We can talk about her in front of Jeanne, who's one of the family. Things aren't going well between her and her husband."

Emile kept his eyes on his mother. He saw her lips moving. Sounds reached him. He understood what they meant. But what concern of his was all this?

"She came to see me last month, and the moment she arrived she flung herself into my arms and burst into tears."

Geraldine was able to burst into tears. He could not.

"The children are grown up now. Patrick's at the university. He wants to be a chemist. Marie-Lou isn't officially engaged, but she's got a serious boy friend. Serge will be finishing high school this year and is sure to pass. They've got everything they need to be happy. They're all fit and well. Fernand is earning a good salary."

"Geraldine's a fool to make such a fuss over a little thing like that," her father grumbled.

"Fernand has a mistress. Your sister's convinced that one of these days he'll want to get a divorce and marry her. She's a beautiful young woman, who works in the same office as he does. A real Parisian, you know. Now Fernand dines out more often than not. He often doesn't even come home at night on the pretext of having some urgent work to get done. She says he's no longer the same man. Even with his children he's cold and standoffish. I tried to cheer her up. I pointed to your father, who was smoking his cigarette out in the yard. 'Look at that man,' I said to her. 'He's still with me. But if I were to count up all the girls he's run after. . . .'"

The old man threw out his chest, his eyes twinkling, and went into the kitchen to pour himself another glass.

"I don't want to bore you with Geraldine's troubles when I see you so seldom. How's your work going, Jeanne?"

"I'm still translating English and American books."

"You don't find it too tiring?"

There were two or three customers. The girl was quite capable of serving them, so his mother was content to keep an eye on things from a distance.

Nearly an hour went by in the same way. Emile said hardly anything. It was his parents, particularly his mother, who did most of the talking.

"You remember Madame Chevalier, who used to wear a white hat all the year round? She died of cancer last week. She was eighty-eight."

Scraps of the past like that, which cropped up haphazardly in an old woman's mind. His father listened, sitting astride his rush-bottomed chair.

"Don't you get worn out living in Paris? It's a long time since I've been there, but life seems to have become hellish. And all these scuffles with the police! I hope, at least, it's been quiet in your neighborhood?"

"Yes."

They were pressed to eat apricot tarts. Emile did not want to, but he made this sacrifice for the sake of peace. When they left, he was at the end of his tether, and he secretly vowed, as he had done on previous occasions, that he would never go back there again.

The courtyard, with its pale yellow walls, was drenched in sunshine, yet for him everything was drenched in greyness. It was as if he were inhaling the dust of a past he cared nothing for.

Was there anything he really did care for? He would have found that difficult to answer. Jeanne? It was practical to live with her. He was used to it. He would be vexed if she died.

They made their way to the station, walking rather slowly because of the sun that beat down on them.

"They're good people," Jeanne said softly. "You're lucky to have parents like those two."

He nodded.

"When you think I don't even know what's become of my mother . . ."

"Of course."

There were only a few people on the platform, and they waited patiently for the train to arrive.

It was Emile who suggested:

"What do you say to our taking a little trip next month?"

"Where to?"

"Italy, for instance. You don't know Italy. Neither do I. I don't want to get stuck in the same place for all of our vacation.

"It wouldn't be too expensive?"

"Not more expensive than, say, Les Sables-d'Olonne. There are organized tours by plane and bus, but I don't like that idea."

"Nor do I."

When they got back to Rue du Faubourg-Saint-Jacques, there was a moving van once again in front of the house.

It was not the same one. Pieces of furniture were not being piled into it but being unloaded and taken up to the third floor. The door of the apartment opposite theirs was open. They could hear the voices of a man and a woman but could not see them.

Emile opened an atlas.

"The most logical thing to do would be to start with Florence, then go on to Rome, Milan, and Venice."

"Let me see."

They were both bending over the map, and there was a semblance of intimacy between them that lasted perhaps half a minute. Emile was tracing their intended route with the tip of his finger. He was sitting down, and for a moment, as Jeanne leaned forward, her bosom brushed against him.

"Sorry."

He had not noticed it, and he wondered what she was apologizing for.

"If we have any time left over and it isn't too hot, we might even go to Naples and Sicily."

He said all this in a calm, even voice, without any tremor of excitement. It was she who was the more interested of the two.

"How long do you think of staying away?"

"Three weeks? A month? It's entirely up to you. When we've had enough of it, we'll come back."

"Do you think we'll be able to find rooms?"

"One always manages to find one in the end. It's not as if we were a large family."

The following week, he went to a travel agency on Boulevard Saint-Michel and brought back all the folders and brochures about Italy. Several announced cruises that went as far as the Black Sea.

"That's a trip we might take another time."

His employer, Paul Jodet, had rented a villa on the outskirts of Deauville, for his wife had no desire either to isolate herself or to mingle with the common herd. Their son did not go with them. He and two of his friends had chartered a yacht, and they planned to sail around Spain. Each of them was taking a pretty girl along with him.

The Virieus left on the tenth of July. Emile had been to see his sister. He had found her thinner and nervously tense, but she had not spoken to him about her husband's affair with the other woman. Neither of them had known what to say to each other. They had never been very intimate. They had not been friends, as an only brother and sister so often are.

"What about you? I suppose you're all going to the shore?"

"I don't know yet. Fernand hasn't said anything about it to me. You're looking very well."

He felt heavier than he had last summer. No doubt, as he got older, he would get fatter and fatter, like his mother.

They had taken berths in a sleeping car. The train was full. They arrived in Florence at ten in the morning, and the city was already like a furnace. There was a hotel opposite the station, but its appearance suggested that it was expensive.

Emile went up to a Cook's representative in uniform and a gold-braided cap who was standing in the center of the concourse.

"Excuse me," he said.

"May I help you, sir?"

"Do you know of a good hotel? Clean and comfortable, but not too expensive."

"Haven't you reserved rooms? You should have done so at one of our Paris offices."

He fumbled in his pockets and hunted through a number of folders.

"Try this one. It's not far from the Duomo and has only just been opened."

Emile produced a note from his wallet and handed it to him. Was it enough? Was it too much?

"How much did you give him?"

"Ten francs."

They took a taxi, for their two suitcases were quite heavy. "Albergo del Ponte Vecchio."

The man at the little desk was surprised that they had not made reservations in advance. He spoke French fluently. He leafed through the register, unhooked a key, and summoned a porter in a red uniform to take them up to their room.

The elevator deposited them on the third floor. Their room number was 301. The shutters were closed to keep it cool and the porter opened them.

The furniture was so new that it seemed to have come straight from the shop.

"Would you like this one?"

"Yes. You may bring up the luggage."

By great good luck, there were twin beds. They took cold showers and went down to lunch. Now they could see the Ponte Vecchio, with its shops on both sides. In the afternoon they strolled about and went into the Uffizi Gallery. Emile was familiar with the names of the painters, from Giotto to Botticelli and Ghirlandaio.

It so happened that he had read several books on the Renaissance and on the lives of the famous characters of the period. The paintings as such made no particular appeal to him, but he was interested in the lives of the painters and in the persons depicted.

In front of certain pictures more than thirty people stood listening to a guide who repeated his commentary in several languages.

When she heard French or English spoken, Jeanne listened. Then she looked at the illustrated catalogue they had bought when they came in.

They visited the black and white cathedral and fed the pigeons.

After two hours Emile's feet were burning and painful.

"Shall we go back to the hotel?"

"Are you tired?"

"It's my feet."

They could not find their way back at once through the mass of traffic with buses full of tourists weaving in and out.

"Tomorrow we must go to Fiesole. It's a monastery where Fra Angelico once lived, and there are still some monks living there. From there one can see the whole city and part of Tuscany."

There was no enthusiasm in his voice. He spoke exactly as he would have spoken of his sore feet. Jeanne, on the contrary, was indefatigable.

"You ought to buy a guidebook to Florence and its sights so that we can read it this evening."

In the end, they unearthed a bookshop, and Emile bought two guidebooks so that they could each have a copy.

When they got back to their room, he felt a sharp pain at the base of his skull, and he knew that his migraines were beginning again. He did not complain. He was used to them. He took his medicine and, having removed his shoes, lay down on his bed and waited.

"Not feeling well?"

"A bit of a headache."

"Is it one of your bad ones?"

"I don't know yet."

He gazed at her, standing there in the bedroom, wearing a flowered dress, and wondered what she was doing there with him. There was no intimacy between them, no mutual understanding. They had lived the same life, side by side, for so many years, without even knowing each other.

Was it the same with other married couples? His sister's husband had given her three children. They had brought them up together. They were a little over forty, and now he had taken it into his head to get a divorce because he had met a younger and more exciting woman. Did that not mean that they had never understood each other either?

And Jeanne's mother, who had as good as given her child to her sister in order to follow her lover to the United States?

He was not depressed. To be so, he would have had to know what it was to be gay. But he had never been gay. He never laughed, and he never complained either. He led the life he had chosen to live. Their holiday abroad had hardly begun, and already he was rejoicing in the thought of returning to his glass cage and the smell of hot oil and molten lead.

They stayed four days in Florence, and during those four days he never stopped having pains in his head. When he mentioned them to a doctor, the doctor looked at him with knitted brows, as if perplexed, examined him, and gave him a prescription without offering him any explanation of his symptoms.

To get to Rome, they traveled by bus. The passengers were of many nationalities, and here, too, there was a polyglot guide to point out the most interesting features of the country they passed through.

A young girl sitting near them took notes in shorthand. A man with a blotchy face refreshed himself from time to time from a silver hip flask that must have contained brandy or whisky.

Nearly all the men had removed their jackets, and their shirts had large stains of sweat under the arms.

Before leaving Florence, Emile had taken care to go to the station and consult the Cook's representative, who gave him the address of a hotel in Rome.

The hotel was not luxurious, but it was comfortable. Its only drawback was that it looked out on a square that was endlessly swarming with traffic, and the cars were perpetually emitting loud blasts from their horns.

Here, too, they bought a guidebook and a plan of the city. They visited almost everything. The most expensive thing was the taxis. It was even hotter than in Florence, and they stopped by every fountain they found on their way.

"How's your head?"

"A bit better."

What he did not say was that the sun made him giddy, and he was nervous about crossing the Roman streets with their heavy traffic. Often he was on the point of taking Jeanne's arm but could not bring himself to make a gesture so unprecedented as to be almost unthinkable.

In the restaurants they ordered without always knowing what was going to be brought to them. Luckily, many of the waiters understood English, and then it was Jeanne who did the ordering.

"Are we going to Naples?"

Out of bravado he said:

"Why not?"

Was it not he who had suggested this trip? He did not want to appear less courageous than she. His head was already full of all kinds of mental images, jostling each other, some in shadow, others in blinding light.

They went to Pompeii. In the streets of the ancient city there was a positive procession of people coming from all quarters of the globe. They had to follow the crowd. It was only with great difficulty that they were able to stop now and then for a moment.

In Rome it had been hotter than in Florence.

In Naples it was hotter than in Rome.

What was the point of going to Palermo? It was a long detour, and the heat would no doubt be suffocating.

On the fourth day they took the night train to Venice.

Chapter III

THEIR hotel was situated in a little square beside a canal whose stagnant water had an evil smell. He came across similar squares all over the city. The façades of their buildings were painted red or pink. In his memory, they were mostly red.

In the streets, which were too narrow for cars, it was cool. Whichever one they took, they would suddenly emerge on the Piazza San Marco, where hundreds of men in shirt sleeves, women in light dresses or shorts, little boys and girls, all milled about and stared at each other.

Nearly all the men had cameras slung around their necks. They paid no attention to him, so he was able to stare at them.

He did so with amazement. They were his fellow human beings, but he could see no resemblance to himself in them. What is more, he regarded them as his enemies. He resented their being there; he hated them for being themselves, for behaving differently from himself, for smiling and laughing, for taking in the sunlight, the surroundings, the sights and sounds through every pore of their skin.

They stayed five days in Venice. They saw everything there was to see, always accompanied by a flock of human beings, and in the end Virieu was walking straight ahead of him with the fixed stare and uncertain step of a somnambulist.

Jeanne followed him. She managed never to lose him in the crowd, which was something of a feat. She did not complain of being tired. Her feet did not hurt her. The heat did not bother her.

They went for a trip in a gondola, passing under a great number of bridges and through some of the wider canals. Motorboats skimmed past them and made their small craft rock.

When at last they were back in the train, he collapsed on his seat with a sigh of relief.

"Have you got a headache?"

"No."

He might just as well have said "Yes." It was not a violent pain but a dull, persistent ache that had never left him since Florence. He had seldom had the feeling of being so utterly alone in life.

Everywhere in Italy he was a stranger. But was he not just as much a stranger in Paris? And even in his own apartment?

True, it was not his own. It had been acquired by Jeanne's former husband. He lived among another man's furniture, in a home another man had set up in the expectation of spending a long life in it. In fact, nothing in the apartment belonged to him except one of the twin beds—the one on the right. Jeanne and he had each paid half of the television set. The dishwasher, too.

They arrived at the Gare de Lyon at eleven at night, took a taxi, and at last, to their relief, they were back on Rue du Faubourg-Saint-Jacques, which at this hour was almost empty. When they reached their floor, they heard music and voices. The new neighbors were watching television.

This disturbed him. Anything that was new and unusual disturbed him, as if the entire world was conspiring against him.

He knew it was not true, but the idea did not displease him; neither did the idea of his solitude. He was not like other people, and this gave him a certain sense of pride.

"Did you enjoy your trip?"

She did not say "our trip."

He said "Yes," so as not to hurt her feelings. And, after all, perhaps it was true, at any rate, partly.

He still had five days of his vacation left. He began, the next day, by sleeping till ten in the morning, when Jeanne had long been busy at her typewriter in the living room.

He felt like dawdling about, for the pleasure of doing nothing, thinking about nothing, letting himself sink into a kind of mental fog. After his shower he nearly got back into his pajamas and dressing gown, but he had never done such a thing and did not dare create a precedent. He got dressed as usual, except that he did not put on his jacket.

The telephone rang. He went to answer it.

"Yes. Virieu speaking."

"This is Fernand."

It could only be his sister's husband, for he did not know any other Fernand.

"I've called you several times the last few days, Emile. I didn't know when you were coming back."

Lamark had been the first to address him by his Christian name, and Emile had, of course, been obliged to do the same. This embarrassed him. Familiarity did not come easily to him. For him, Fernand Lamark was a stranger who had happened to marry his sister.

"Did you have a good time in Italy?"

"Yes."

"It wasn't too hot?"

"It was rather hot. Especially in Naples."

"Did you go to Venice?"

"Yes."

"I believe my wife talked to you before you left."

"What about?"

"About her and me."

"She said things weren't going too well."

"I want to talk to you, too. Could we meet this afternoon?"

"Come and see me here."

"I'd rather we met somewhere else. I'd prefer to talk to you without your wife being there."

"Where do you want me to go?"

"You know the Coq d'Or, the *brasserie* on Boulevard Montparnasse?"

"I know it by sight."

"Four o'clock, if that suits you?"

"Right."

He did not like his brother-in-law. It is true that he did not really like anyone. Perhaps he had a vague kind of comradely feeling for Jeanne.

"That was Fernand," he told her. "He wants to see me this afternoon."

"Do you think they're going to be divorced?"

"I've no idea. It's none of my business."

He went for a stroll in the neighborhood, stopping now and then at a little fruit and vegetable barrow. It had a pleasant smell. It would have been perfect if most of the barrow women had not stared at him.

These women were his enemies, too. Are not all human beings enemies of the solitary man?

He was the solitary man, and they were aware of it. His look, his whole bearing bore no resemblance to theirs. He lived in a world of his own; in his eyes, these people he encountered were only shadows.

When he returned home, lunch was ready, and, as always, the two of them had it alone.

"The girl across the way came and asked me if she could borrow some salt."

He did not understand. Then he remembered their new neighbors.

"They've only just moved in, and in all the flurry she forgot the salt. She didn't want to have to get dressed just to go out and buy some. She looks very young and has a strong Alsatian accent."

He received this item of news with complete indifference. After lunch he toyed with the idea of taking a siesta, but he was not in the habit of doing so, and, as far as possible, he avoided doing anything unusual.

It would have been absurd for him to go to Rue du Saint-Gothard, as he would have liked to do, and sit down for a while in his glass cage. He was on vacation. There was nothing for him to do at the printing firm. He thought of the crowds packing the trains and airplanes and filling the hotels, of the bodies lying by the thousands on the beaches.

Paris was almost deserted, for in their neighborhood there was nothing to attract sight-seeing tourists.

He went into a café and sat there drinking mineral water till it was time to go and meet Lamark. Then he made his way to Boulevard Montparnasse, cursing his brother-in-law for ruining his afternoon.

The Coq d'Or was a large place. It was divided all along the walls into booths, rather like boxes in a theater. He saw Fernand at once, signaling to him from one of these boxes.

He seemed tired. His breath smelled strongly of alcohol, and his gaze was slightly unfocused.

"Nice of you to come. Sit down. What will you drink?"

"A glass of beer."

"Waiter! A beer and a double whisky."

He waited till the drinks had arrived.

"How's Jeanne?"

"Very well."

Emile knew that they had made unkind jokes about him when he had married Jeanne. They must have said:

"He's gone out of his way to find the ugliest woman he could."

And someone must have added:

"At least they make a well-matched couple. Let's only hope they have no children."

"Geraldine must have told you I was thinking of getting a divorce."

"She did vaguely mention it to me."

"It's true. I was in love with your sister once, but that's nearly twenty years ago. We were both young. She had a childish look that appealed to me. She was rather like a pretty doll."

He gave a derisive laugh.

"Now the doll's got wrinkles, and her one idea is to spend her evenings at home. But in my job that's impossible. I have to get out and about to meet people."

Emile stared at him impassively, but Fernand, who was getting fuddled, little suspected that though his brother-in-law was looking straight at him, he hardly saw him.

"Here's to you! Listen, I'll give you just one little example of what she's like these days. I've only to order one whisky and she gives me hell. In the old days she used to drink glass for glass with me. Many's the time I've had to undress her and put her to bed. And she used to be the one who was always wanting to go out."

What could Emile have said in reply?

"The children are grown up and off our hands. Haven't I the right to think of myself? I've worked hard all my life. I've given all four of them a pleasant, easy life."

He had drunk so much whisky that he could no longer articulate clearly and kept slurring his words.

"When you marry young, you don't know what you'll do twenty years later. You don't even know what you'll be like. Your sister's hardly interested in sex any more. Whereas I feel at the height of my powers."

Emile continued to stare at him, without offering any comments.

"I was very fond of Geraldine, but it was never a grand passion. That kind of passion is something I've never experienced till these last few months. I don't know if you know what it's like."

"No."

"Her name's Lise Bourdet, and she's about thirty. She has one of the most important jobs in the firm I work for. So I see her every day, although we're not in the same office. Well, every morning I pace up and down in front of the building, watching for her little yellow car to arrive. The moment I see it, my heart begins to pound, and my hands tremble with impatience. If she looks tired or worried, I question her anxiously. I know it's absurd, but I just can't help it. She answers, 'I'm just the same as I am any other day, Fernand. Perhaps I'm not as well made up.' Do you understand that?"

"No."

He could not see himself scrutinizing Jeanne's features and wondering if she was tired or worried. She was as she was, once and for all. He accepted her that way, even if age had not improved her appearance.

"Ten or twenty time a day, I find some excuse for going into her office. She laughs. She says the others make fun of me, but I don't care. I need to see her. I'm always wanting to touch her, to make sure she's there, that it's really she, that she's really mine. Even when I've spent the night with her, in the morning I can't believe she really loves me. It seems too impossible to be true. Don't look at me like that, Emile. I've got to tell you all this, otherwise you wouldn't understand. Of course Geraldine understood at once. It isn't the first time I've had a mistress. There've been some who've lasted three days, and a few who've lasted as much as three or four weeks. She imagined that this time it would be four weeks. Then she saw that it showed no signs of stopping. If I had to stay at home in the evening, I was like an animal in a cage. I felt like smashing the television set she was always watching. At times I could have smashed up the whole place.

"The other night, I poured myself a drink. She looked at me with the usual disgusted expression, and I said to her:

" 'Listen, Geraldine, I've got something awfully important to say to you.'

" 'Not when you're in this state.'

" 'I'm perfectly sound in my mind, and I know what I'm saying. I respect you. You've been my wife for twenty years, and you've given me three children.'

" 'Leave the children out of this, will you?'

" 'There's nothing disgraceful about being in love. They'll never have any cause to be ashamed of me. I respect you, and I don't want to deceive you any more, coming back and sleeping here when I've just left another woman's bed.'

" 'That's quite enough.'

" 'We must deal with it like sensible grown-up people and look at the situation dispassionately.'

" 'Go to bed. That's enough for tonight.' "

He gulped down the rest of his whisky and turned toward Emile.

"That's the sort of reception I get from her. When I mention the word divorce, it's even worse and she goes and locks herself in our bedroom. In the last ten days I've had to sleep twice on the living-room sofa, and my daughter Marie-Louise asked me what I was doing there. Waiter! Another of the same!"

"Not for me."

"Not for him."

He closed his eyes for a moment and appeared to be about to fall asleep. At this time of day, the *brasserie* was almost empty inside, and most of the customers were out on the terrace in the shade of the orange awning.

"Even if I succeed in persuading her to divorce me, things won't be easy because of the alimony and the allowances for the children. For I'm leaving her the children. She'll automatically get the custody of them. All I shall ask is to see them regularly."

He took a drink, coughed, and his eyes turned moist.

"You must have some money, since you and your wife both earn a good salary and you've hardly any expenses."

Emile stiffened and did not reply.

"I've always had a very well-paid job, but we spent everything we earned. That place of ours in the valley of Chevreuse, Les Glaïeuls, cost me a lot. My car cost nearly twenty thousand francs. Our evenings out were expensive, too, and it wasn't any cheaper entertaining at home. Then it was essential to my status for my wife to be well dressed. One fondly imagines that it will go on forever."

It was cool in the *brasserie,* which had wood paneling reaching two-thirds of the way up its walls. The proprietor stood in the middle of the alley between the tables with his hands behind his back, keeping a watchful eye on the comings and goings of the waiters.

Emile knew what this was all leading up to, but he had not the courage to cut short the interview.

"You can't understand how I love her. I don't know if I ought to wish the same thing to happen to you. It's wonderful, and at the same time it's terrible. Nothing else in the whole world matters. If I were told that after a year with her I'd be forced to commit suicide, I wouldn't hesitate. You've absolutely got to talk to your sister and advise her to be reasonable. She has confidence in you."

"No."

"What do you mean?"

"That Geraldine has never had any confidence in me. She looks on me as a fool and a failure—a man not quite like other men."

"Nonetheless, you're the only person she can lean on."

"She doesn't need to lean on anyone."

"Does that mean she's strong?"

"Yes."

"All the same, I implore you to go and see her."

"I will, but only on condition of not giving her any advice."

"I'll leave her the apartment and the furniture. If she wants it badly, I'll leave her the car. I'll leave her Les Glaïeuls, too. In other words, I'll keep nothing for myself. She doesn't care about my financial situation."

Virieu still did not blanch. He watched and listened to Fernand as if he were an actor playing a scene. He was quite willing to believe that his brother-in-law was in love. But what did that expression mean? And was not Fernand deliberately dramatizing the situation in order to bolster up his own self-esteem?

What would become of him in six months or six years?

He was impatient now to have done with these confidences, which seemed to him indecent.

"For the first few months, I shall find it difficult to support two households. For, of course, I don't want to sponge on Lise. I figure I'll need, say, ten thousand francs, to tide me over."

Emile's features were stony, and his eyes totally expressionless.

"Can you lend me that?"

"No."

Fernand was shaken by this emphatic "No."

"Are you sure? You must certainly have money put by. I'll give you the same interest as the bank."

"I can't."

"Why?"

"Because I have never lent anyone money, and I never will."

"And if it was your sister who asked you to?"

"I'd give her the same answer."

Fernand sighed. He emptied his glass at one gulp. His hand was shaking.

"I'll have to find someone else. You were the person I immediately thought of."

Emile said nothing. His brother-in-law's face was very red.

"You'll go and see my wife anyway?"

"I've already said I would."

"You despise me, don't you?"

"No. I don't despise anyone."

"Then what *do* you think of me?"

"I don't think anything."

"You're about the same age as I am. What's happened to me might happen to you one of these days. Then you'll know what passion is."

"I'll see when the time comes."

He stood up. He had had enough of all this. He needed to get back into the fresh air, even into the blazing sunshine.

"Good-bye for now, Fernand."

"Thanks all the same."

His brother-in-law remained slumped on the seat and called the waiter. To pay for his drinks? To order another?

If he had come in his car, he would have difficulty in driving home. If he had walked, he would no doubt take the métro. It would be better for him not to go to his office in the Champs-Elysées in the state he was in.

Emile had no pity for him. He asked no pity for himself from anyone, and he felt none for anyone.

He walked rather slowly along the sidewalk so as not to get into a sweat. He would go and see his sister tomorrow morning in order to get it over with. For her, and no doubt for Fernand, too, it was a catastrophe. He did not know this Lise who, no doubt unintentionally, had caused it.

He did not believe in passions. He believed neither in men nor in women. He loved nobody. "Love" was a word that was not in his vocabulary.

When he returned home, Jeanne, who was sitting at her typewriter, turned around to look at him.

"Bad news?"

"Yes and no. Fernand wants a divorce. It doesn't look as if my sister will agree to it. But she won't make things any better for herself by going on living with a man who'll soon come to hate her."

"Have you seen your sister, too?"

"I'm seeing her tomorrow."

He went straight to the telephone and called her.

"Is that Geraldine?"

"No. It's Marie-Lou. I'll call Mamma. It's Uncle Emile, isn't it?"

"Yes."

"One moment. Mamma! Uncle Emile wants to speak to you."

Geraldine must have been in another room, for Marie-Lou had to shout.

"How are you?" he asked mechanically.

"All right. And you?"

The voice was tired but not dramatic.

"I'd like to see you."

"Has Fernand phoned you?"

"Yes."

"Have you seen him?"

"I've just left him."

"Did he weep on your shoulder and talk about his grand passion?"

"May I go to see you tomorrow morning, say about half past ten?"

"Not later, because I have an appointment at half past eleven with my lawyer."

"Would you rather I came at ten?"

"Yes. Make it ten."

It was not the voice of a helpless, distraught woman. She had always known what she wanted in spite of her apparent weakness.

"Was it he who asked you to come and see me?"

"I should have come in any case. He wanted to entrust me with a mission on his behalf, but I refused to undertake it."

"About the divorce, of course?"

"Yes."

"Did you have a good trip?"

"Not bad."

"You didn't find it too hot?"

"Sometimes. Particularly in Naples. Till tomorrow."

It did not embarrass him to talk about his family affairs in front of Jeanne, but he did not take the trouble to explain the situation beyond what she could gather for herself from his telephone conversation with Geraldine. In marrying her, he had provided himself with a witness.

They were together nearly all the time he was not working in his glass cage. When he got up in the morning, she was there. She was aware of all his moods.

In spite of this, he did not confide in her. It was not that he did not trust her. It was simply because he felt no need to.

In conversations with her, too, he was in the habit of replying simply "Yes" or "No." He had a way of calmly enunciating these monosyllables without adding any other words, which made people look at him curiously and a little uneasily.

What was the point of explaining things? People were not worth the trouble, so why bother? Most of the time, they would not have understood, even if he had.

"I suppose you don't want me to go with you?" Jeanne asked, still seated at her typewriter.

And it was his eternal:

"No."

He read the book on Venice that he had bought in Italy, although when he was actually in the city he had done no more than idly leaf through its pages. At that moment, for him, the tour was already over, and he had very nearly never set foot in a gondola.

They had a cold supper, as they often did on summer evenings. They had opened the two windows of the living room and could feel a faint breeze on their faces.

After supper they watched television, which was showing a popular play transmitted directly from the theater.

"Your sister can still make a new life for herself."

She had no need to receive confidences. She had understood. And she had weighed her words carefully before venturing to make this remark. Was it not, for her, an indirect way of coming closer to him? What it meant was:

"I'm here. When you feel the need to talk, you'll always find me here to listen. I'm more your wife or, if you prefer it, your friend, than you think."

He was glad that he had married her. With the passing of time, she might have become intolerable and tried to take a greater place in his life.

For him, things were very satisfactory as they were. She was there, and that sufficed him.

"Good night, Emile."

"Good night, Jeanne."

He thought about his sister for maybe ten minutes; then he fell asleep till he woke the next morning to the clicking of the typewriter.

He took the métro to Boulevard Diderot and rang his sister's doorbell. The maid was busy cleaning the living room, and Geraldine said:

"Come into the bedroom, so that we won't hear the vacuum cleaner."

The bed was not yet made, and entering like this into the intimate life of a married couple, even a couple like them, shocked him.

"I'm not going to ask you what Fernand said to you. I know his jeremiads by heart. He's not a bad man. Only he's remained a spoiled child, and he's selfish, as children are. Everything's got to go according to his wishes, and if his wants aren't immediately satisfied, he flies off the handle. He's attractive to women, no doubt about that. After our marriage, he went for nearly two years without looking at another woman. Then he had an affair with a Malaysian girl who worked for a time in his advertising firm. 'Don't be afraid,' he told me. 'It won't create a precedent. In three or four days I'll have broken it off.' It was true. There were others in due course, and his longest affair lasted a month.

It was during that month that he stayed out twice all night. When he came home in the morning to shave he was like a dog with its tail between its legs, and he humbly begged my pardon. So you see I know what he's like."

"Yes."

What else could he say?

"This time, it's more serious. They've been lovers for three months now. He hardly ever comes home to meals. My children asked me: 'Do you really believe Papa's working all that time, even at night?' And Patrick, who saw them in a night club in Saint-Germain-des-Prés, said: 'You bet he isn't!' Marie-Lou asked: 'Will he come back for good?' I said: 'I don't know, my dears.' And it was true. With him, one can never know."

Emile gazed at her with his expressionless eyes.

"Has he talked of coming back?"

"No."

"Do you believe he will?"

"No. He can't get a divorce without my consent. That's why I'm going this morning to see a lawyer who's a friend of ours. He knows us both well. We've often been out together, with him and his wife. It's Maître Delteil. Do you know him?"

"No."

"I just can't make up my mind what to do. If I divorce him as he asks, he'll be ruined. He's always been extravagant. He earns a good salary, but we've always spent the money as fast as he made it. I don't even know whether or not there's a mortgage on Les Glaïeuls. He'd never consent to live on this woman. He's got three children to support, not to mention alimony. In a pinch, I could do without, though it wouldn't be easy at my age to go back to work. Who can say if I'd be able to find a job?"

Virieu listened to her with a face as inscrutable as a Buddha's. Problems and feelings of this kind seemed to have no place in his universe.

His sister went on, still calmly and judicially:

"On the other hand, if I refuse to divorce him, he'll

make my life impossible. He's become a tormented man who no longer has any clear idea of what's real or unreal. As long as he has hopes that I will, he still doesn't actually hate me. But when he sees that he's getting nowhere, he'll go completely to pieces. He's already drinking from morning to night. If he goes on like that, he'll risk losing his job. As to this Lise, whom I don't know, she may get tired of him. What should I do then, with a human wreck on my hands? Advise me, Emile. What ought I to do?"

"I don't know."

"Is that all you can find to say?"

"Yes."

"Do you at least understand the situation?"

"Yes."

"To divorce or not to divorce; that's the whole question."

"Yes."

"What would you do in my place?"

"It's difficult for me to put myself in your place."

"Very well. I think I've wasted my time. I hoped you'd give me some advice, but I realize it's too much to ask of you."

He got up.

"It must be nearly time for your appointment with the lawyer."

"Let's hope he'll be a little more talkative. Good-bye, Emile. Remember me to Jeanne."

Geraldine had aged. She had fine wrinkles at the corners of her lips and two deep grooves on either side of her nostrils. It was not so long ago that she had been a little girl.

Did she say the same thing to herself when she looked at him? They had grown up together without any real intimacy ever having been established between them. When they first came to Paris, they had almost lost sight of each other, since each of them had to make a living on his own.

It had all happened so quickly. Now they were middle-aged people. In a few years they would become old ones.

He walked as far as the Gare de Lyon, where he went into the station restaurant and had coffee. What would he himself do if what had happened to his sister were to happen to him? Suppose Jeanne, for some reason or other, were to ask for a divorce? The furniture, except for one of the twin beds, belonged to her. Their apartment was in her name, for she had already had it in her first husband's time.

There would be nothing for him to do but to take his suitcase and go in search of a place to stay. The idea of finding himself alone again in the evenings in a hotel room filled him with gloom.

He crossed the bridge and walked along by the Seine embankment, his mind a whirl of chaotic thoughts. At a certain moment, he heard himself muttering:

"I'd kill her."

He had not thought it. They were merely words that had automatically sprung to his lips, but which meant nothing. Nevertheless, as he said it, he had clenched his fists.

He was a peaceable man, endowed with an extraordinary capacity for inertia. He would, he knew quite well, do nothing at all. He would go on shutting himself up every morning in his glass cage and correcting sets of proofs.

He walked all the way home, slowly, looking every now and then into a shop window. Did he even see the objects displayed in it? Did there exist the same barrier between himself and things as between himself and human beings?

He knew that he was not quite like other people. But was it not he who was rational and the others who were milling about in a vacuum?

When he reached home, he walked upstairs instead of taking the elevator. He heard voices in the apartment opposite theirs. It was the new tenants, both of whom had German accents, especially the woman. She had a voice like a little girl's and a slight lisp.

He turned the handle of his door and pushed it open. Jeanne was in the kitchen, preparing the lunch. Suddenly, without knowing why, he felt guilty about her. Not really guilty. He felt indebted to her.

She gave him more than he gave her. If she was rather ugly, that was not her fault. It was he who had chosen her ugly, with full knowledge of what he was doing.

As they got older, they would both get uglier. Perhaps one day they might have a little dog?

This idea of a little dog attracted him. Jeanne stayed at home nearly all day, and it would be company for her.

He joined her in the kitchen.

"What would you say to a little dog?"

"Do you want to buy one, or has someone offered you one?"

"It's an idea that's just occurred to me."

"Why, of course, I'd love one."

"You've never said so."

"I thought you didn't like animals."

"I've nothing against them."

"What breed were you thinking of?"

"I don't know. It's for you to choose."

"How about a miniature poodle?"

"I don't know them. I don't know anything about dogs or cats."

They had their lunch, and Jeanne's face was more animated than usual. Normally, it was never she who proposed an outing. Nevertheless, as she passed him the fruit bowl, she could not help asking:

"Are you doing anything this afternoon?"

"Nothing special."

"Would it bore you if we went to see about the dog?"

"No. But where?"

He had not the faintest idea of the places where they sold dogs.

"There's a pet shop at the Porte d'Orléans. I've seen it advertised in the paper."

"So you were already thinking about it."

"I didn't dare to hope."

Perhaps other couples would have embraced each other. Not these two. It was years since they had done such a thing.

"I'll do my dishes quickly."

63

He settled down in his armchair and read the paper. Tomorrow, life, real life, would begin again: at nine o'clock he would go into his glass cage, and the transparent walls would separate him from human beings.

They took a taxi because they did not know exactly where the pet shop was. The driver, luckily, did.

In one window was a fox terrier bitch with seven puppies who kept climbing up on her body and sliding off. Several people were watching the sight with doting admiration.

In the other window a great Dane and an Alsatian were separated by a partition.

They went inside. The room was a very long one. A parrot chained to a perch was screeching raucously. Chained to another perch was a little reddish-brown monkey of a species unknown to Emile.

"What may I do for you and the lady, sir?" asked the salesman. He wore white overalls and had rumpled hair.

Jeanne gave her husband an embarrassed look, as if to say:

"*You* tell him."

"My wife would like a miniature poodle."

"I have some three-months-old ones that I can thoroughly recommend. I've got only two of them left."

He led them to the far end of the room, which had rows of cages on both sides. The poodles, who were lying together, half opened their eyes.

"They've been inoculated against distemper. We guarantee all the animals we sell. Would you prefer a dog or a bitch?"

Once again, Jeanne turned to her husband.

"A dog," he said.

He was thinking that all the dogs in the neighborhood would follow them if they bought a bitch.

The puppies were black. One of them had a white patch on its chest. The salesman took it out of the cage, and the puppy let itself be handled like a baby. Set down on the tiled floor, it stayed exactly where it had been put and looked up at Emile and Jeanne, wagging its stump of a tail.

"Isn't it a dear?"

Emile had never thought his wife would say such a thing.

"I'd like to hold it."

"Please do."

She lifted it up and cradled it in her arms like a baby. The puppy let her do as she liked with it. It seemed a trifle sleepy. A red spaniel in the next cage watched the proceedings, giving little yaps.

"What's he called?"

"He hasn't a name yet. It's for you to give him one."

Once again she looked at Emile as if it were a matter for urgent decision.

"Is he housebroken?"

"He might forget himself once or twice, especially when he finds himself in new surroundings. I suppose you don't mean to keep him chained up?"

"Certainly not!" said Jeanne indignantly.

"You must take him out at least twice a day. Do you live in town?"

"On Rue du Faubourg-Saint-Jacques."

"For the country I'd have recommended a hardier breed."

"How much is he?"

"Five hundred francs. Of course he has a pedigree. His parents have won several prizes at poodle shows."

She put the dog down on the ground.

"What do you think?"

She was about to open her handbag, but Emile had already taken his checkbook out of his pocket.

"Half each, then."

"No."

It was he who had first suggested buying a dog, and it was he who insisted on paying for it.

"You must come and choose a collar and leash and a muzzle. I've some very efficient feeding bowls that can't be overturned. I'll also recommend the best kind of dog food for him. This brand is especially good for puppies."

By the time they had finished, the bill amounted to nearly six hundred francs. The collar and leash were red, which made an effective contrast with his black coat.

For the first few yards the poodle let himself be dragged along, and Jeanne kept stopping to stroke him. Finally, she picked him up and carried him.

"Would you like me to call a taxi?"

"Yes, please."

Along with their Italian trip, this was the most outstanding event of their married life.

"What are we going to call him?"

"I don't know."

He had never tried to find a name for a dog.

"It mustn't sound silly."

"Jeannot?" he suggested.

"That would seem as if he were called after me."

"Quite logical, since he's your dog."

The puppy had gone to sleep. His stomach was still as round as a barrel.

"Bébé?"

"And what about when he's five or six?"

"Not Kiki, though."

"No."

They both went on trying to think of a name for the dog. Only the day before, such a scene would have been unthinkable.

"Why not Noris?"

She repeated the name several times.

"That sounds good."

Then she spoke to the dog.

"Noris . . . Noris . . ."

He opened his eyes as if he had understood.

The concierge was standing behind the glazed door of her lodge. They felt guilty about not having told her of their intention to buy a dog. It was Jeanne who opened the door.

"He's sweet, isn't he?"

"Is he yours?"

She was a woman of thirty-five whose husband, a truck driver, had been killed in an accident. She had remained fresh and vivacious.

"He won't grow too big?"

"He's a miniature poodle."

"Because if it were a big dog, you'd have trouble with the landlord. It would be better if you didn't take the elevator."

They went upstairs to their apartment, and Noris, after having sat for some time on his haunches looking up at them, went off to sniff around the walls.

Chapter IV

Ⅰⴝ was a little after nine o'clock. The two of them, each sitting in his own armchair, were watching a televised debate on highways, when suddenly there was a noise on the landing, followed by a series of violent, impatient knocks on their door.

They stared at each other, while the dog, who was lying on a cushion that had already become his own special one, lifted his head and yapped.

Emile got up and went to the door, feeling somewhat apprehensive. His wife followed him with her eyes.

When he opened it, he found himself confronted with an obviously intoxicated Fernand, who was so unsteady on his legs that he was leaning against the doorframe.

He could hardly see straight. He lurched forward, tottered across the room, and collapsed in Virieu's armchair. Jeanne had switched off the television. She was standing up, ready to make a tactful exit, but Fernand stopped her.

"You needn't go. I don't mind talking in front of you. I'd talk in front of the whole world if it were here."

His eyelids were inflamed and there were red patches on his cheeks. His jacket was crumpled.

"You were right, my dear brother-in-law. Lise doesn't want to have anything more to do with me."

Emile refrained from telling him that he had foretold nothing of the kind, for it would have been useless. It was obvious that Fernand was obsessed by a single idea.

He went on, after a jeering laugh:

"In other words, she's ditched me!"

He gave another jeering laugh.

"Did you come by car?"

"What car?"

"Yours."

"I don't even know where it is. I've left it somewhere, but I can't remember where. Have you any whisky?"

"No. There should be a little brandy left."

"Give me the brandy."

He had reached the point where it was wiser not to oppose him. All that he and Jeanne risked was to see their brother-in-law fall asleep and spend the night in the armchair or on the floor.

"She's a bitch. But what a beautiful bitch, damn her!"

Jeanne gave him a glass of brandy, and he swallowed it at one gulp.

"Give me another. I need to pull myself together. It's *the* day of my life, do you realize that, you two? You've never lived through a day like this because you're quiet, respectable people."

He turned to Emile.

"I bet you've never slept with any other woman but your wife. Well, I've not only slept with other women, but I'm in love with one. I say love because I know what it is, and I know what I'm talking about, even if I'm a bit tight."

He tried to stand up but fell back into the armchair.

"Where've you put the brandy, Jeanne?" he asked, addressing her by name for the first time.

She looked at her husband as if to ask what she ought to do, and he signaled to her to refill the glass. At the stage Lamark had reached, it no longer mattered how much more he drank.

"I've been to see the lawyer. His name's Delteil . . . Jean Delteil. He's a pal, and we've often got drunk together. Which doesn't prevent him from being a swine. He received me like a stranger, like an ordinary client. I said to him:

" 'Well, Jean old man, have you seen my future ex-wife?'

"And he replied:

" 'You shouldn't have been drinking on a day like today.'

"Hear that? A day like today!

" 'And the divorce?' I asked him. 'When's this divorce to be?'

"Whereupon he treated me to a long lecture. In the first place, Geraldine was a thoroughly nice woman and as much his friend as I was. In the second, I had three children."

Emile had finally sat down on the edge of a chair. He gazed at his brother-in-law with a completely expressionless face. He himself had never been drunk. Jeanne would much rather have left the room, but she realized it was wiser not to annoy Fernand.

The latter looked at them in turn.

"Have you two lost your tongues?"

"We've nothing to say. You're doing all the talking."

"Perhaps I ought not to talk? Is that what you mean? According to you, I ought to suffer in silence."

He appeared to be defying them, and his eyes wandered in search of the bottle of brandy.

"Whatever's that?"

He pointed to Noris, who had got up from his cushion and was sniffing his legs.

"It's our dog."

"So you've actually got a dog! Wonders will never cease! Can't you have children like everyone else?"

He gave a derisive chuckle, as if he were rather pleased with himself.

"D'you know what's emerged from Delteil's lecture? The pair of them have been doing accounts, my legal friend and my legal wife. For I've the misfortune to have a legal wife. Right! Where was I? Oh, yes, they've been totting up the bill. So much per child. It's Patrick who's the most expensive item because he's studying for his degree. He won't earn his own living for another four or five years. So much for Marie-Lou. So much for Serge. And on top of all that, my wife must be provided for.

" 'Even if she finds a job, Fernand,' the lawyer told me, 'the judge will award her alimony.'

"They can pull a trick like that on me. I can starve, for all they care. I'm the villain of the piece, you see, the swine who deserts his pure, devoted wife and his innocent children and reduces them to beggary. So that's that! No, I haven't finished. My head's a bit muddled."

"Did you come on foot?"

"On foot!" he repeated, as if he had not understood the first time. "Wait while I think. I stopped a taxi and asked the driver to. . . . The man was a swine and wouldn't take me. Said he didn't want to have me being sick all over his cab. I walked. I went into a bar to piss. May I have another drink?"

When Jeanne had filled his glass, he went on:

"Now it's all come back to me. The accounts . . . that's it. He'd written it all out neatly on a piece of paper. So much for Patrick, so much . . . I haven't told you this already, have I? Tell me frankly. Don't think I'm drunk. I'm worked up. It's not the same thing. And I'll tell you why I'm worked up. Listen to this, Emile. And you listen too, Jeanne. You may get some tips that'll come in useful if ever my brother-in-law falls in love.

"The accounts . . . Well now, if you add up what I'd

have to pay and subtract the total from what I earn, I'd have three or four hundred francs left. Precisely. I don't know if that's the law, but that's my dear old friend Delteil's idea of it.

"Three hundred francs to keep a wife on! Perhaps that's what your dog's going to cost you. Lise has a good job, I know. But a self-respecting husband can't depend on what his wife earns to keep the pot boiling."

He was silent for a while, looking once more from one to the other, as if challenging them to raise an objection.

"Twenty solid years we've been married, your sister and I. Since they're doing accounts, try to reckon up how much I've spent on her during that time. Suppose I had all that money in my pocket now?"

They could hear the muffled sound of their neighbors' television coming from the apartment across the way.

"I've seen Lise. . . ."

He paused a moment for dramatic effect.

"I've seen her as plain as I see you. I went to her department, where everyone stared at me. I ran into the big boss and I asked him:

" 'How goes it, you old swine?"

"He didn't dare contradict me. He really is a swine. Then I barged into Lise's office.

" 'Come on,' I said to her. 'I've got to talk to you. We'll go and have a drink at the Tom-Tom.'

"It's a bar almost next door to our offices. She realized at once that she'd better come. Otherwise I might have smashed up the place."

Emile stared at him fixedly and wondered whether his brother-in-law was as drunk as he wanted to appear.

"We sat right at the back so that Joseph, the bartender, shouldn't hear us.

" 'I've been to see the lawyer.'

" 'I hope he's persuaded you against it.'

" 'Because you're on their side, too?'

"She took my hand under the table.

" 'Listen, Fernand, we've discussed it from every angle. You know as well as I do that this marriage is impossible. Besides, what more would we get from it? You see me whenever you want to. Your wife leaves you quite free.' "

Jeanne finally sat down in her armchair.

"Have you taken that in, Emile? In other words, it's thanks to your sister that I'm able to sleep with Lise. I told her about the accounts, Delteil's famous accounts.

" 'I knew it,' she sighed. 'You'd much better go to bed, either at home or at my place. If you'd rather go to mine, I'll give you the key.'

"She was already rummaging in her handbag.

" 'As if I were the plumber,' I said.

"She didn't get the point. I signaled to Joseph to fill up our glasses.

" 'And suppose I get a divorce anyway?'

" 'That wouldn't be a reason to marry you. Be reasonable, Fernand. We're very fond of each other. For the moment we enjoy spending part of our time together. That doesn't mean. . . .'

" 'That doesn't mean what?'

" 'That we'd make a good married couple.'

" 'You refuse?'

" 'Yes.'

" 'Is that definite?'

" 'Yes.'

" 'You refuse because I won't have any money left?'

" 'I refuse because in a few weeks you'd be very unhappy.'

" 'So you know better than I do what I'll be like in a few weeks? All right, then *I'll* tell *you* something. You're a whore like all the rest, Lise. What's more, before me, you slept with the boss, who's sixty-five and a swine. Try to deny it.'

" 'I've nothing more to say to you, Fernand. Nothing more at all. I don't bear you any ill will. Our affair is over for both of us. Tomorrow, at the office, I'll say good morning to you, just as I say it to the others.'

"She got up, and before she made her way to the door, edging in and out of the tables, she whispered:

" 'Good luck!'

"What d'you say to that?"

Their only response was silence, a heavy, embarrassed silence. He looked at them with a disgusted expression, then got up, not without difficulty, and made a pretense of giving the dog a kick to push it away, while Jeanne watched anxiously, ready to intervene.

"Right! I see you're on their side. I'll be off. I won't waste your precious time any longer. I apologize to my pretty sister-in-law"—he gave a broad grin to emphasize the irony—"for having stripped myself naked in front of you. Oh, yes. I've stripped myself naked. . . . Morally naked . . . More naked than naked. I love her still, and I'll shout it from all the housetops. Farewell. Be happy, all three of you."

He bent down to grab the dog or to stroke it, but Jeanne had already snatched it up in her arms.

"Farewell to you, too, brother-in-law. And thanks for the brandy. It'd do you good to get tight from time to time."

He zigzagged toward the door, overturned a chair, made an attempt to pick it up but realized that this would be dangerous. He opened the door and disappeared into the elevator, loudly clanging the gates.

Emile and Jeanne stared at each other. It was she who finally found her tongue. She said in a hesitant voice:

"Fundamentally, he's an unhappy man."

Her husband made no reply. It was ten o'clock. Their television program was over, and, in any case, they were not interested in highways. They moved automatically toward the bedroom, as on any other evening.

"What shall we do with Noris?"

"Noris?"

"The dog. If we leave him in the living room in the dark, he might be frightened. You mustn't forget he's still a baby dog. To feel we were in the same room would reassure him."

Norris's cushion was placed in a corner of the bedroom between the bathroom wall and the chest of drawers.

They went into the bathroom in turn to undress. Jeanne gave the dog a good-night kiss, and it licked her cheek.

A little later she switched off the bedside lamp.

"Good night, Emile."

"Good night, Jeanne."

He did not go to sleep at once. Fernand's visit had troubled him. His conscience was uneasy. Yet he had done nothing wrong. It was not his business to help his brother-in-law. In any case, no help was possible.

And yet Fernand had come to them as a suppliant. For he had been pleading for sympathy in spite of his drunkenness. Under all his bluster, he had been almost imploring someone to stretch out a friendly hand to him.

Emile had been content to stare at him stonily and remain silent.

What was Fernand going to do? No doubt rush into the first bar he saw. Drunk as he was, he would go on drinking, and perhaps in an hour or two the police would pick him up on the sidewalk.

He was a poor specimen. For years he had lived in a fool's paradise. He was gay, full of life, kindly, and even affectionate, toward everyone.

This did not stop him from being a weakling, incapable of managing his own life, still less that of his wife and children.

A weakling. It was on this word that Emile drifted off into sleep, wondering whether he, too, were not a weakling. Luckily, his thoughts were already hazy and distorted.

"Emile."

He vaguely heard someone uttering his name in the distance.

"Emile."

Next, someone was shaking his shoulder. Jeanne had got out of bed and was standing beside him.

"The telephone."

"What time is it?"

"Can't you hear it ringing in the other room?"

He had always been a heavy sleeper and difficult to wake up. He hunted for his slippers under the bed and went into the living room, where the telephone was still ringing.

"Sorry to wake you up, Emile."

He recognized his sister's voice. She sounded very agitated.

"Have you seen him tonight?"

"Yes. He came here."

"He's just gone out, and I'm frightened for him. He turned up just as I was getting ready to go to bed. He was so drunk that he knocked over my dressing table and broke the lamp. I had to grope in the dark to find the switch for the ceiling light. He looked awful. He was breathing very hard, and his eyes were bloodshot.

" 'Return to the fold!' he announced and then burst out laughing. He was completely drunk.

" 'Don't make a noise, because of the children.'

" 'They'll have to know one day what their father was like. For I presume I *am* their father?'

" 'Be quiet, Fernand.'

" 'So I'm not even allowed to speak in my own home now? I pay the rent. I paid for the furniture. I paid for that dressing gown you're wearing. I've spent my life paying, and if I dare utter a word, I'm told to shut up.'

" 'What's happened?'

" 'What's happened is that I no longer want a divorce. I can't afford it. Delteil's made me realize that. He's dotted the i's. And when those fellows dot the i's, they make a thorough job of it. . . . You saw him. . . . The two of you discussed figures. . . . Lise has dotted the i's too. . . .'

"All the time he was talking, he kept opening and shutting drawers, as if he were looking for something. . . . He frightened me. . . . What did he say to *you* when you saw him?"

"He talked all the time about Lise, about you and the

children, about himself. Most of all about himself. He insisted on my giving him brandy, and I didn't dare refuse for fear he'd make a row and disturb the neighbors."

His sister went on:

"I couldn't make him stop talking.

" 'Three hundred francs, that's all I'll have left,' he said. Then he laughed again, a bitter laugh that was more like a sob. 'But you know that as well as I do. You plotted it all between you, you and my old friend Delteil.'

"I tried to calm him down, but he wouldn't let me get a word in edgeways.

" 'He must have imagined that I'd come trotting home meekly to my lawful bed. . . . Lise thought that too.'

"At one moment I thought he was going to collapse on the bed and burst into tears. I heard footsteps in the hall, then the door opened and Patrick came in in his pajamas, rubbing the sleep from his eyes.

" 'What on earth are you two doing, making such a row?'

" 'You're right, son. . . . I'll speak lower. . . . I'll even go away.'

"I made a sign to Patrick to leave, and he went back to bed.

" 'You see?'

" 'See what? That I'm not wanted here? I realize that, believe me! Sure, I'll go away. But I don't have a centime left on me.'

" 'I've some money in my bag.'

"I had two hundred francs and some change. I gave him the whole lot.

" 'Thank you, Madame Lamark. You're very kind, Madame Lamark. I promise not to bother you any more.'

" 'Are you going to her?'

" 'In my opinion, that's none of your business. I promise you in any case that there won't be a divorce. And that I shan't remarry. Once is enough, don't you agree, Madame Lamark?'

"He nearly fell over backwards, and I shouldn't have been able to lift him up. He's heavy.

" 'Farewell!'

" 'Be careful, Fernand. Perhaps it would be better if you stayed here. Did you come in the car?'

" 'No.'

" 'Where is it?'

"He made a vague gesture.

" 'Somewhere in the universe.'

" 'Did you have an accident?'

" 'Once again, no . . . Farewell!'

"He staggered to the front door, managed to open it, and slammed it behind him. I went out on the landing and saw him on the floor below going down the stairs, holding on to the banisters. I'm frightened, Emile."

"Frightened of what?"

"In the state he's in, it's impossible to know what he'll do. What do you think I ought to do?"

"You can't run after him. He'll go on drinking. God knows where he'll finally pass out. Probably in the street, in which case the police will pick him up."

"It hurt me to see him like that. I've often seen him drunk but never like this. It was as if I could see through his drunkenness and read his thoughts, as if there were something he desperately wanted to say and couldn't."

"Go back to bed."

"I shan't sleep."

"Take a sleeping pill. You must have some in your medicine chest."

"I don't know. I don't know anything any more. It's all happened too quickly. Do you think this woman has really thrown him over?"

"It's what he told us, too."

"Sorry to have awakened you. Go back to sleep. And forgive me for having dragged you out of bed at this hour."

"What time is it?"

"One o'clock. Good night, Emile."

78

"Good night, Geraldine."

When he got back to their bedroom, Jeanne was waiting for him in her dressing gown, with the dog in her arms.

He fell into a restless sleep, and for a moment he thought he must be dreaming when he heard the telephone ringing. Was he not just reliving the first part of the night in his sleep?

Jeanne had already switched on the bedside lamp. Putting on his purple dressing gown, he went sulkily into the living room.

"Hello!" he growled. "Hello!"

"Listen, Emile . . ."

There was a silence, during which he could distinctly hear her gasping for breath.

"He's dead."

Virieu's first thought was an accident. In the state he was in, Fernand might have got himself run over by a car. Or he might have been killed in a drunken brawl.

"The police superintendent has just telephoned me. He's put a bullet through his head. They found him dead on the landing of that woman's apartment. I don't dare go there alone, and Patrick's too young to come with me. It's 33B, Rue du Berri."

"Is it necessary for you to go there?"

"It seems I have to identify the body before they take it to the Medico-Legal Institute."

"It's always so in cases of suicide. I know that from correcting the proofs of detective novels. There has to be a post-mortem. It's the law."

"Be quiet! I don't want to think about it. I'll get dressed quickly and leap into a taxi. I'll wait for you outside on the sidewalk if I get there before you. If you're there first, wait till I arrive."

He hung up the receiver. It was half past three in the morning. Jeanne was standing outside the bedroom door.

"He's put a bullet through his head."

"Where did it happen?"

"On the landing of his mistress's apartment."

He was calm and inscrutable.

"I shall have to go there because Geraldine's afraid to go up alone."

He got dressed. Then he went softly down the stairs, gave his name at the concierge's lodge and asked her to pull the cord that opened the street door from inside. He had to walk as far as Boulevard Montparnasse before he found a taxi. A night club was still open and he could hear music coming from it.

The first thing he saw on Rue du Berri was the Medico-Legal Institute van outside the apartment house, with a policeman standing by it. There were no curious onlookers. Any prostitute about in the street hurried on toward the Champs-Elysées, having no desire to linger in a place where she felt something sinister was going on.

The policeman asked him:

"Are you from the press?"

"No."

"What are you waiting for?"

"My sister."

"Does your sister live in this apartment house?"

"The dead man is her husband."

"Pardon me, sir. That's different."

He soon saw the taxi come around the corner of the street, and Geraldine alighted from it.

"Will you pay for me? I gave him all I had this evening, I mean yesterday evening, because it's morning now."

He paid the fare and gave the change to his sister, who slipped it into her handbag.

"I don't know what I ought to have done, Emile. I have the feeling that it's all my fault, that I didn't know how to deal with him."

They went up in the elevator and found themselves in a blaze of light. There were tenants in their night clothes on the staircase.

Fernand was lying in the middle of the landing, on the red carpet, and half his face seemed to have been removed. A man with a camera, obviously a police photographer, who had been bending over the body, stood up.

"Don't you think I've got enough now?"

"I think so. You can go."

Another man, who had taken the time to dress carefully, went up to Geraldine.

"Madame Lamark, I presume?"

"Yes. I'm with my brother."

The police superintendent mechanically shook hands with Emile.

"All my sympathy. I apologize for having disturbed you in the middle of the night. In any case, it's only a formality. Do you identify the dead man as your husband?"

"It is definitely my husband."

It was a wonder how she managed to stay upright. She was deathly pale, and her hands were gripping her bag so tightly that the knuckles were white. She was swaying on her feet, staring at a young woman in an orange dressing gown who was standing in the doorway of the apartment.

"Do you recognize his writing too?"

The superintendent handed her a card that bore the address of a night club on Rue de Ponthieu. On the back of it were two words, scribbled in pencil, *Forgive me*.

"It was certainly he who wrote that."

She stared again at the young woman in orange with curiosity rather than hostility. To which of the two was this last message addressed? And why was it here that he had wanted to die?

The superintendent turned to the stretcher bearers.

"You can take him away."

Two of the curious spectators, an elderly couple, went back to the floor above. The rest wanted to see everything to the end. One of the police inspectors lit a cigarette.

A strong smell of alcohol hung over the landing. There was a great deal of blood on the floor and some fragments of brains.

"May I clean up?" asked a woman who must be the concierge.

"Yes."

The superintendent turned to Geraldine again.

"I'd like you to be at my office at eleven. There are a few routine questions I have to put to you."

"I'll be there."

She had not shed a tear, but her hands were trembling, and she felt icy cold. Lise, who had disappeared for a moment, returned with a glass which she offered her in the simplest, most natural way, without a trace of ostentation.

"It's rum."

She drank it as if she did not know what she was doing. As for Emile, he was as calm as the superintendent and the stretcher bearers. Up to the last moment he had kept his eyes fixed on his brother-in-law's corpse, and no one would have known what he was thinking.

"Come in and sit down a moment."

Geraldine found the invitation quite natural and followed Lise into the apartment, which had a faint but all-pervasive smell of perfume. The rooms were quite large, decorated in pinks and greys, and most of the furniture was white.

"Do sit down."

"Did he try to see you? Did he knock on your door?"

"No. I was fast asleep when the sound of a shot woke me up with a start. I didn't realize at once that it was here. I went to the window to look out in the street when I heard voices on the landing. It was the tenants from the floor below."

She was as tall and willowy as a fashion model, with lustrous black hair and regular features. Her face was covered with cold cream, but this did not seem to embarrass her. The two women gazed at each other with mutual curiosity. Lise went on:

"He was still holding the weapon in his hand. It was a revolver."

82

"With a very short barrel?"

"Yes."

"It's his. I was wondering tonight what he was looking for in the chest of drawers. He's had that revolver for years without ever using it. He always kept it hidden under his shirts because of the children."

She spoke mechanically as if she were talking for the sake of talking.

"Did he go to see you tonight?" asked Lise.

"Yes."

"Did he tell you it was all over between us?"

"Yes."

"What did he mean to do?"

"I don't know exactly. He was so terribly drunk."

"About what time did he leave you?"

"About one o'clock in the morning."

"In that case, he must have gone on drinking. His last message is written on the card of a night club on Rue de Ponthieu."

Emile gazed at them alternately, but his face remained inscrutable.

"Won't you have a drink?" Lise asked him.

"No, thank you."

"I'm going to have one myself."

There was a bar in the corner. She went over to it and poured herself a whisky.

"For you, too?" she asked Geraldine.

"Yes, please."

She was as limp as a rag.

"It's my fault," Geraldine muttered, as if she were talking to herself or as if she were in the confessional. "I've only just realized it. He had nowhere to go but back home. Only he didn't want to admit it. He had his pride. He wouldn't talk to me about anything but you. I can't remember clearly any more. I think I'm getting it all mixed up. If I'd told him to stay, he'd have stayed. He'd have gone to bed and fallen asleep at once."

"You mustn't blame yourself too much. I was hard, too, when I was with him this afternoon. He made me leave the office and go out to a bar with him. He was already drunk, and if I'd refused, he'd have become violent. It was his visit to that lawyer—I can't remember his name—that had made him get into such a state. He stormed about it so loudly that I had to ask him to keep his voice down; the people at the other tables were turning around and staring at us."

She mechanically lit a cigarette and offered the silver box to the other two. Emile refused, but Geraldine took one and smoked it in quick, nervous puffs.

"I have to go to the police station in the morning. They asked me to come at eleven."

"I have to be there before you, at ten."

Emile remained rigidly aloof, hearing the women's voices but not listening to what they were saying. Dressed in black, as he nearly always was, he looked extraordinarily incongruous sitting in an armchair upholstered in white satin. He felt completely out of place in these ultrafeminine surroundings.

"Are you feeling a little better?" Lise asked Geraldine.

"Yes, thank you."

"I want to be frank with you. I'd have agreed to go on seeing him as we've been doing lately, but I didn't want to live with him and break up your marriage. I told him so. I explained to him that the whole idea was impossible, but the more I said, the more he refused to listen to reason."

"I know. That's just like him."

"I'd have done anything for this not to have happened. And why did he choose to kill himself outside my door? I wondered for a moment if it wasn't a kind of revenge."

"I don't know."

"You're not feeling well, are you?"

"I'm all right. Just suddenly terribly tired. I don't want to think any more."

"Do you feel strong enough to go back home?"

Even the cold cream on Lise's face could not detract

from its beauty. She had long legs, and as she was sitting with them crossed, the folds of her dressing gown had fallen apart, revealing their flawless shape. Looking at her, Emile could see why his brother-in-law had found this woman sexually desirable.

"Yes, thank you. I'll be quite all right," said Geraldine, rising to her feet. "My brother will see me home."

She moved toward the door, and Lise followed her, her tall body undulating as she walked.

"If you need me for anything, no matter what . . ."

At first Geraldine could manage no more than a forced smile in response. Then she hesitated and finally brought herself to hold out her hand.

"Wait while I ring for the elevator."

When it came up, Geraldine and her brother got into it, and little by little Lise vanished from their sight.

"I understand Fernand . . ."

Emile looked at her inquiringly.

"She's beautiful. So much more beautiful than me! In any case, I was never really beautiful, as you well know. Even as a little girl. And, after three children, my figure's ruined. He loved her. It was she whom he asked to forgive him before he died."

They found themselves back in the street and started to walk toward the Champs-Elysées to get a taxi there.

"Do you think he'd have stayed with me if I'd kept him at home tonight?"

"No."

"Why?"

"Out of pride."

"Or perhaps he loved her too much."

"That's a word I don't understand."

"What word? Love?"

"Yes."

"Don't you believe such a thing exists?"

"No."

"Don't you love your wife?"

"No."

She gave him a disapproving look as they were passing under a street lamp.

"*I* believe in it. I loved him."

An empty taxi came by, and Emile hailed it.

"Boulevard Diderot."

Virieu could not remember ever having been out so late at night. It seemed to him that the sky was already lighter to the east of Paris. Geraldine was obviously cold, but he was incapable of making the simple gesture of putting his arm around her shoulders.

There was some traffic around the Gare de Lyon. Boulevard Diderot was deserted.

"What number?"

"Eighty-two."

He paid the fare.

"I'll come up with you. I want to make sure you're all right."

It was a lot, coming from him. Once in the apartment, they switched on the light in the living room and bedroom. The bedclothes were flung back in disorder, as Geraldine had left them when she had been called away.

"Get undressed. I'll wait in the other room."

"Talk to me a little first. I'm afraid to be alone. Just say anything."

"Unfortunately, I've nothing to say. I think it couldn't have gone on much longer, that it was bound to come to an end."

"Between her and him?"

"Between the three of you."

"What am I going to tell the children?"

"The truth. They'll read it in the papers."

Patrick burst into the living room, barefooted and tousled, with an angry frown on his face.

"What's all this commotion about? It's impossible to get a wink of sleep in this place tonight."

"Sit down, Patrick. I'm afraid I have some bad news for you. It's about your father."

"Has he had a car accident?"

"No. He's dead."

"But why? He wasn't ill."

"He killed himself. Not long after he left here tonight, he shot himself through the head."

The young man stared at her in disbelief. Then he stared at his uncle, who, in his black suit, must have looked to him like a bird of ill omen.

"Where is he?"

"The police have taken his body to the Medico-Legal Institute."

"Why didn't they bring it back here?"

"It's the rule in cases of suicide."

"Where did he do it?"

Geraldine turned to her brother, mutely imploring him to take over. She was at the end of her tether. It was a miracle that she had managed to hold out as long as she had. Emile was reluctantly forced to say something to Patrick.

"You knew, didn't you, that your father had a mistress?"

"Not only one. He's had several."

"With this last one, it was more serious. Anyway, it will all be in the papers tomorrow."

"Was it at her place that he. . .?"

"Outside the door of her apartment."

"I suppose she'd said she was through with him?"

"I think he didn't want to leave you all, but he couldn't make up his mind to leave her either."

"Poor Papa," sighed the young man, getting up from his chair. He went over and kissed his mother's forehead.

"Poor Mama," he said, stroking it.

Then, suddenly, his mind turned to something else.

"I have an important lecture tomorrow morning. May I go to it?"

"Yes, of course."

"You won't need me for anything?"

Marie-Lou appeared in turn, rubbing her eyelids.

"What's going on in here?"

Her brother went straight to the point.

"Father's dead."

"Oh, *no!*"

"He's shot himself."

"Has he really done that, Mamma?"

"Yes."

"But why?"

"We don't know for certain."

"What are we going to do?"

"We shall see later on."

"You'll have to get a job, won't you? And perhaps we'll have to move because the rent here's so high and we may not be able to afford it."

The third and youngest child, Serge, was the only one who had remained asleep.

Emile stood up to go.

"Have you any kind of sleeping pill?"

"Yes. Fernand used to take them."

"Take one yourself and get to bed as soon as possible. Tomorrow I'll be at work all morning and afternoon. If there's anything you want, give me a ring."

He cast a last look at all three of them, standing, as if rooted to the spot, in the brightly lit living room, then made his way to the door and let himself out.

Neither of the children had shed a tear. One of them had talked about the lecture he was anxious not to miss that morning. The other had been preoccupied with the future and the cost of the apartment.

Outside there was no taxi in sight, so he walked slowly toward the station, automatically keeping close to the houses. He could hear the noise of engines shunting, and by now the sky was a pinkish yellow.

There was already quite a crowd of people milling to and fro under the high glass roof of the station.

As he had done less than twenty-four hours earlier, when he was killing time before meeting Fernand at the Coq d'Or, he went and had coffee at the station restaurant.

He would have found it hard to say what he was think-ing. Not for an instant tonight had he felt any touch of sorrow or pity.

He had stared fixedly at his brother-in-law's tall figure lying on the landing, and perhaps in the depths of himself what he had felt for Fernand was something like envy.

Chapter V

WHEN he woke up at seven, he did not hear the clicking of the typewriter. It was as if something were missing. Any change in his habits gave him a general sense of uneasiness. In the living room, he found Jeanne watching the dog eating its prepared food, occasionally looking up to make sure that she was not going to take it away.

They exchanged their usual laconic "Good morning." Then he went into the kitchen to pour himself his first cup of coffee and drank it.

His vacation was over at last. So was the drama of his brother-in-law.

He took his shower, shaved and dressed in the way that he always did, performing each step in his toilet in precisely the same order and allotting the same time to each.

He had slept very little, and he was feeling the effects of his disturbed night when he arrived at the breakfast table to find his two boiled eggs, bread and butter and second cup of coffee waiting for him.

"You don't know yet when he's being buried?"

"No."

"Perhaps the Lamarks have a family vault?"

"I don't know."

"Was he born in Paris?"

"I haven't the faintest idea. All I remember is that he lost his parents a long while ago."

At half past eight he took his black hat and set off for work. As he emerged from his own apartment, a young woman, almost a child, carrying a shopping bag, came out at the same time from the opposite apartment. She stood still for a moment, startled, then made a sign to him to go ahead of her.

"After you," he said.

She, too, gazed at him curiously. It was seldom that anyone looked at him as they would at any passer-by, perhaps because of his prominent, expressionless eyes, perhaps because of the lack of any animation in his face. He gave the impression of being mentally retarded or of a man completely turned in upon himself.

The young woman had white skin as fine as a baby's. Her straw-colored hair was curly, and her wide mouth had a natural tendency to smile.

As she walked along the street in the early-morning sunshine, she kept stopping to look in shop windows and, since they were going in the same direction, he appeared to be following her. Twice she turned round, and both times she seemed surprised to find him close behind her.

Finally, she went into the butcher's where they themselves bought their meat, and he continued on his way, not without a tinge of regret.

Soon he was back on Rue du Saint-Gothard, relieved to hear once again the clatter of the printing presses and smell the good smell of hot oil and lead. He went up to the second floor. Monsieur Jodet was already in his office and dictating his letters. He stood up and shook Virieu's hand with unusual solemnity.

"All my sympathy. I heard the news on the radio. It must have been a sudden impulse."

Emile's only response was a noncommittal shrug.

"How did your vacation in Italy go?"

"All right."

He did not put himself out for his employer any more than for anyone else. However he added:

"It was hot."

"It's been hot everywhere, even at Deauville. You'll see two sets of proofs on your desk. The pamphlet's the more urgent."

At last he found himself back in his corner, his cage which protected him against everything that existed outside. After so many years he hardly knew the names of the men who worked in the pressroom, right under his eyes. There was one whose face was always very red and another who had a clubfoot. The foreman had grey hair and a crew cut. Usually, when he looked at them, it was with a blank, unseeing stare.

The morning passed peacefully and pleasantly. He worked slowly, with meticulous care. Being a purist, he had a horror of grammatical errors. He had found them even in the texts of schoolteachers and university professors.

Almost at once, it was lunchtime. The dog yapped and nipped the bottoms of his trousers, wagging its stump of a tail.

"You can't imagine how nice it is not to feel alone. He knows me already. He watches me inquisitively while I'm working, as if he wonders what on earth I'm doing."

The radio was on in the apartment opposite. Had the husband returned?

For lunch there were grey shrimps, bread and butter, veal chops with spinach, followed by a fresh-fruit salad.

"No one's telephoned?"

"No."

As he left home again, he automatically glanced at the door opposite. The radio was still on.

About three o'clock the telephone rang in his cage.

"It's for you, Monsieur Virieu."

It was Geraldine, and he was vexed with her for intruding like this into his private world.

"You're not too tired, Emile?"

"How about you?"

"I had to cope with the children. I haven't slept much. At eleven I went to see the police superintendent. He asked me a lot of questions. He particularly wanted to know if I knew about Fernand's affair and if he'd told me he wanted a divorce.

" 'They've held the post-mortem,' he told me. 'There's no doubt that it's a case of suicide.'

"I asked him: 'What else could it have been?'

" 'We always have to consider the possibility of murder.'

" 'But who might have had any motive for killing him?'

"He said, with a faint smile: 'There were two women in his life, weren't there?'

"I don't know what that woman Lise told him. Personally, I preferred to tell him the truth, including the fact that Fernand was dead drunk.

" 'We knew that from the post-mortem. He had drunk an incredible amount of alcohol.'

"But that's not why I'm telephoning. He told me that the body was at my disposal. I've never had to deal with a death before, but the undertakers said to leave it all to them, and one of their representatives has been here to discuss all the arrangements. The funeral will be on Friday."

"At what time?"

"I don't know yet. I had a phone call from Papa; he'd heard the news on the radio. He asked me if he ought to come to the funeral. It would mean he'd have to close the shop for the day, so I told him not to. I'll call you when I know more details."

For him the whole affair was over, and the rest was a mere formality. The body no longer had any connection with Fernand. It was no more than a piece of dead flesh that might have been anyone's.

An hour later, his sister telephoned again, and this time he showed his impatience.

"I'm sorry, Emile. I know you're working. But I've no one else to turn to."

"Say what you want to say."

He nearly added: "But say it quickly."

"The undertaker's been here again, and I think everything's arranged. They're not taking the body to their mortuary chapel but bringing it back here. It will be here in an hour. They'll put it in the guest room. Because of his wound, they'll close the coffin at once. The man asked me if we had any religious affiliation. I said we had both been brought up Catholics but that since our marriage, and even before, we were no longer practicing ones. However, he thought it would be better, for the sake of our friends, to have some kind of church ceremony. So there will be an Absolution at Notre-Dame-de-Bercy at ten on Friday morning. The most difficult problem was to find a cemetery. There's no room in any Paris cemetery anywhere near here. The only available plot the undertakers could find is in the cemetery at Bagneux, so it will have to be there. Somehow I don't like the idea."

"Why not?"

"I don't know. It seems so strange to have to bury him out in a suburb. I'm sure I've never so much as set foot in Bagneux."

He went on listening, but absent-mindedly. He heard her talking about whether there should be five cars or six cars, about the people who would come in their own.

"The telephone never stops ringing. And of course I have to answer."

Fernand Lamark was no longer anything but the cause of innumerable worries.

"Do you think I ought to send an announcement to that woman?"

"Why not?"

"Doesn't it seem rather odd?"

"She worked in the same firm as he did. She'll probably come with his other colleagues."

"Right. I'll try not to disturb you again. You'll come on Friday?"

"Yes."

"And your wife too?"

"Certainly."

Jeanne probably liked funerals. Most women like funerals.

Having hung up the receiver, he heaved a long sigh of relief and got down again to his proofs.

When he informed Jeanne of the date and time of the funeral, she objected:

"But the dog will be left all alone."

"It's bound to happen to him sometimes."

"He's still so young. Aren't you, Noris?"

He could not get used to this name. Every time she said it, he wondered whom she was talking about.

They watched television. It was showing a play that was supposed to be funny. Neither of them laughed, and they went to bed at half past ten.

"Good night, Emile."

"Good night, Jeanne."

How many thousands of times had they murmured those words as they settled down in their separate beds and turned off the light?

The next morning the door opposite opened at the same time as he opened his own. The woman-child smiled at him as one smiles at someone one knows by sight. She was wearing tight grey pants and a thin jumper that revealed tiny pointed breasts.

He followed her as he had the day before. She stopped

before the same windows, went past the butcher's, and entered the delicatessen shop. When he walked past it, she gave another smile, but he could not be sure it was meant for him. There are people to whom smiling comes naturally, who smile at the blue sky, at the multicolored bustling street, or just at their own thoughts.

In his cubicle at the printer's, he avoided thinking of her. He was interested in her only because she was his neighbor on the landing and they went out at the same time in the morning. He was not in love. He was not even physically attracted to her.

He did not know the husband yet. For the past two days he had not heard his voice. Was he away?

When he returned home at the end of the afternoon, he hesitated for a moment in the hall, then went into the concierge's lodge.

"I've noticed that we have some new neighbors."

"Yes. They seem to be a very nice young couple. They've only been married three months. They were born in neighboring villages somewhere near Strasbourg. You'd think she was only a little girl, to look at her. Her husband's a good head and shoulders taller than she is. He's a traveling salesman and goes away twice a week for three days."

He was annoyed with himself for having asked these questions. What concern was it of his? When he reached their landing, the door opposite was half open and the window, too, and the young woman, still dressed as in the morning, was looking at a book of comic strips, with the radio on.

She did not raise her head. He paused only for a moment. Had she opened the door only to create a draft, since it was a stifling day? Or was it for him?

He shrugged his shoulders. No woman had ever been in love with him. Neither had any ever been interested in his movements.

While he was waiting for dinner, which was not due for nearly two hours, he read a book without paying much attention to it.

The funeral was fixed for the following day. After that, the Lamark affair would be over once and for all.

Jeanne said:

"Perhaps we ought to stop in at Boulevard Diderot."

"It seems to be the custom, so I presume Geraldine will expect us to. Have you sent flowers?"

"No."

They went out. A little farther down the street there was a florist's.

"You choose," he said to his wife.

It seemed ludicrous to him to send flowers to a dead man. She naturally chose chrysanthemums. She paid and asked her husband if he had a card with him. Then they took the métro and traveled to their destination without exchanging a word on the way.

There were no black draperies over the street door as there had usually been in his recollection. There was nothing to indicate that there was someone dead in the house. The door of the apartment had been left on the latch to let the visitors enter freely.

Geraldine, who was standing in the living room, saw them arrive and came out into the hall to greet them.

"I was sure you were going to come. I didn't expect so many visits. All his friends have come and quite a lot of people I've never met but whom he must have known."

"Did Lise come too?"

"Yes. She looked at me rather nervously. She was with another woman from the office. She bowed to me and then found her own way to the room where the coffin is. I knew she'd have no difficulty since she'd only to follow the others. Do you know, Emile, all this seems quite unreal to me? I don't feel that he's there, or even that he's dead."

The guest room was full of flowers. The coffin was of light oak with silver-plated handles and ornaments. The two lighted candles at the head of it emitted the sickly smell of hot wax.

"How are the children taking it?"

"They've already got used to the fact that he's dead."

"Are they coming to the funeral?"

"Only Patrick. The younger ones said they'd rather not."

"Are you all right for money?"

"Yes. I went to the bank to cash a check, and they didn't make any difficulties. The insurance agent has been here too. Fernand had taken out a life insurance for a hundred thousand francs. He hadn't told me about it. When we'd just got married, it was only fifty thousand, but when the first child was born he doubled it. If the policy had been signed less than a year ago, I shouldn't have got anything because Fernand committed suicide. I don't understand anything about these matters."

Emile and Jeanne dined alone together as usual. They turned on the television to hear the news. When it was over, it was announced that the next program would be a documentary on Africa.

"What did Geraldine do when she first came to Paris?"

"She was a salesgirl in a shop on Rue Royale."

"She isn't a stenographer?"

"She can type, yes. But she never managed to learn shorthand."

He nearly added:

"She's not very intelligent."

It was true. He saw her once more as she had been in her teens, very popular with the other girls of her age. She was always going around to their houses or entertaining them in her bedroom over the shop. She had had a love affair with a local boy, the son of the proprietor of the radio and record shop. It had been broken off rather dramatically, but she had not used him as a confidant. Luckily, for he had a horror of that role. Though there was only a little more than a year's difference in their ages, there had never been any intimacy between them.

He had been the first to leave home for Paris. She had followed him not long after, but they hardly ever saw each other. For quite a while she had shared a room with another girl in a little hotel near the Gare Montparnasse.

She would certainly be able to find a job. She was still quite smart and attractive.

The documentary was not bad, but it did not finish until a quarter to eleven. Emile was annoyed at having to stay up beyond his usual bedtime. Noris, who was not interested in television, slept all through the program, lying on his stomach with his nose in his cushion.

"Good night, Emile."

"Good night, Jeanne."

Was he happy? Was he unhappy? He did not ask himself that question. He was neither one nor the other. He simply lived, that was all, coping as best he could with his solitude.

Was it others who did not accept him? Or was it he who deliberately kept aloof from them?

Perhaps both. And that went back a long way, to his childhood, when he had never had any friends. The other boys made fun of him and said his eyes were like marbles. They pretended to be afraid of him.

"Look out! Here comes the devil!"

In the end, he had got used to it and derived a kind of bitter satisfaction from it.

"Why don't you go and play outside with the other boys?"

"I don't want to."

What was the good of telling his mother that for them he was the devil? As a young man he did not try to approach girls. They, too, looked at him suspiciously.

In any case, they did not interest him. People did not interest him. He met them in the street and gave them a cursory glance, then hastily looked elsewhere.

He slept till seven, and this time he heard the sound of the typewriter. When he walked through the living room to go and have his cup of coffee in the kitchen, the dog had finished its food and was pushing the bowl about with its nose.

. . .

The church was almost full. True, it was not a large one. They brought in the coffin, covered it with a black pall embroidered with a silver cross, and arranged the wreaths and bunches of flowers around it.

Fernand's chief was there, as well as a good half of his colleagues. In the front pew there were only Geraldine, their son Patrick, in a brown suit, and Emile and Jeanne.

The usher allotted people their places according to their importance. The organ played slow soft music. When it stopped, the priest entered, followed by an acolyte.

There was no Mass, only an Absolution. It was the first time that Emile, who had not set foot in a church since his boyhood, had heard the prayers said in the vernacular.

He listened absent-mindedly. He had missed seeing the girl from the opposite apartment. Seeing her every morning had become a habit.

Lise was there, looking very elegant among the rows of people from the advertising agency. She was the only woman in black. Geraldine had not bought herself a dress for the funeral, but she, too, was wearing a black one, though hers had white trimmings.

"Give us this day our daily bread."

His mind reverted to his brother-in-law as he had seen him four days earlier, dead drunk and endeavoring to make him understand his state of mind. He had not talked of death but of life—life with Lise, of course—and how he was not going to let anyone rob him of it. The word "love" kept recurring all the time.

"I love her, Emile. Do you realize what that means?"

She was there, in the third row. He was there, too, in that sealed-up oak box.

Four hefty men came to carry him away again. The church part was over. There remained only the cemetery. The crowd moved toward the door, preceded by the family.

All four of them got into the first car. Others were put into the cars that followed. Several people had come in their own so that there was quite a cortege of cars following the hearse on the long drive to the cemetery.

As it made its way through Paris and out toward the suburbs, Geraldine talked about how popular Fernand had been with everyone.

"Wherever he went, he always made friends," she said.

Emile spent the afternoon in his glass cage, and when he returned home, his wife, who was correcting the last chapter of her translation, got up to welcome him. She looked slightly embarrassed.

"I had a visitor half an hour ago. The young woman across from us who came once before for some salt. Today, she came to ask us to go and have coffee in their apartment about eight. Her husband is back. He's nearly always away traveling for his firm. I was rather flustered and didn't know what to answer. Finally, I said it depended on you, since you sometimes brought work to do at home. You'd think she was still just a little girl. She could hardly bear to leave Noris, who'd been romping with her and licking her cheeks."

She looked at him, awaiting his answer. She was quite surprised when he said simply:

"We'll go."

"It won't annoy you too much to have your usual routine upset?"

"In any case, we'll have to go there sometime or other. So it might as well be tonight."

He put on his black-framed glasses and settled down in his armchair to read the paper. It was his time for reading the paper. His eyes ran over the lines without always taking them in.

He was surprised. It was probably she who had suggested to her husband that they should ask them in. Why?

It was impossible for him to think that she was in love with him. Then what was her motive? Was it only curiosity, as it was with people who turned to look back at him in the street?

She would have the opportunity to see him close up, to hear him talk. He was impatient without knowing why. He, too, was looking forward to being in her home, to seeing her in her own setting, to listening to her.

They dined a little earlier than usual. Then they crossed the landing to that door which Emile was at last going to enter.

They rang the bell. Immediately she flung the door wide open. She was wearing a flounced pink dress that made her look like a little girl dressed in her Sunday best on the way to church in her village.

"I'm so glad you've come."

She had a rather high-pitched voice, and her Alsatian accent was not unattractive.

"François!" she called. "Come in. My husband won't be a moment."

She took them into the living room, which was the counterpart of theirs. Whereas she herself was so tiny, the man who now appeared was very tall and built like a wrestler. He shook Emile's hand, wringing it so hard that he winced, then bowed to Jeanne.

"Lina's told me how kind you've been to her. She's always forgetting something. Luckily, in the move, she forgot only the salt."

His accent was less marked than his wife's. He had red hair and a thick, coarse-grained skin like the skin of an orange. His eyes were very light.

"Do please sit down."

The furniture was heavy old Alsatian furniture, ornately carved. The armchairs were covered with flowered cretonne. The two doors of the sideboard were painted with hunting scenes in crude bright colors.

Emile had not expected to find the table laid. Four places had been set with dessert plates that had a broad gilt rim. The tablecloth was hand-embroidered in different colored threads. Was it she who had embroidered it?

And in the center stood an enormous cake.

Jeanne felt somewhat awkward and ill at ease. She sat

on the edge of her armchair, clutching her handbag on her lap.

"Have you lived here long?"

Emile let his wife reply:

"Twenty-five years."

"The neighborhood's fun, isn't it? In the morning you see all those little fruit and vegetable barrows along the sidewalk across the street. The tradeswomen call out to you and crack jokes when you go by."

The husband turned to his wife.

"Lina's very fond of the street. She gets more fun out of it than I do, since I'm nearly always away. I represent a company that makes ball bearings, and I have to go and see their customers in the provinces."

"He leaves me all alone," complained Lina. "I hope he'll soon have a settled job, perhaps in the manager's office. I got married to have a man of my own, who'd be with me all the time, not just on Saturdays and Sundays."

It was years and years since Emile had attended a social gathering of this kind. They had occasionally spent an evening with Geraldine and her husband, but the Lamarks had never put themselves out for them. From time to time they had also gone to Etampes, where they had indeed been obliged to eat cake, but where his father received them in his working clothes, with his arms bare, and his mother in her white apron.

"Oh! I've gone and forgotten something again. I ought to have asked you whether you'd rather have tea or coffee?"

Jeanne looked at her husband, who replied:

"A little coffee, if it's no trouble."

"My name's François Keller. I hope you won't mind my asking you yours, now that we're neighbors?"

"Emile Virieu. I'm a proofreader, and I work at a place less than half an hour's walk from here."

The young woman disappeared into the kitchen. She was away for quite a few minutes, and Emile was surprised to find himself casting impatient glances at the door through which she had vanished.

When she returned, she was carrying a silver coffeepot that must have been a wedding present.

"I hear you have a pretty little dog."

"We've had him only a few days."

"Lina's crazy about him. Perhaps I'll have to buy her a dog, too. Not a big one, not one of our Alsatian sheep dogs, who are terrors."

"Will you cut the cake, Franz?"

She must sometimes call him François and sometimes Franz according to circumstances. No doubt Franz was what she called him when they were by themselves.

"You see what women are! I've only just come home after three days on the road and already I'm made to work."

He laughed. His good humor was natural and spontaneous.

"Cream in your coffee?"

"No, thank you."

"How much sugar?"

"Two lumps."

The cups had a gilt rim like the plates. Another wedding present?

She put slices of cake on their plates. Emile noticed that the backs of her hands were covered with freckles.

All this was slightly unreal. Emile was simultaneously aware of a peculiar kind of gratification and of a sense of disquiet.

In the honeycombed houses of Paris there must be tens of thousands of couples like this. In a few months, no doubt, Lina would be pregnant, and he would see her going out to do her shopping with a big belly protruding in front of her. Franz Keller would be as exultant as if he had accomplished some extraordinary feat.

They would have other children. She would take them to school, holding them by the hand.

Would Keller have at last got a settled job so that he no longer had to travel all the week?

"Is it good?"

"Very good."

"It's a recipe of my mother's."

"Did you make it yourself?"

Keller said:

"She's as good at making fancy cakes and pastries as she is at plain cooking. Pity I can't take more advantage of it."

There was a silence. Everyone was eating. Emile was not hungry, and he loathed cakes, having eaten too many of them in his childhood.

"Tomorrow morning we're going off to the country for the weekend."

He asked, out of politeness:

"Where are you going?"

"We don't know. We'll leave Paris by the south. We shan't take the highway but the roads that go through the villages. Perhaps we'll stop somewhere on the banks of the Loire. It all depends. It's great fun to go off casually like this without knowing where you'll end up."

"Another slice?"

"No, thank you. You gave us such big ones."

The windows were open. There was little noise in the street at this hour, and it was slowly getting dark.

"Shall I put the light on?"

The ceiling light was made of an old spinning-wheel with small electric bulbs fixed all around its rim. When it was switched on, they returned to their armchairs.

"Do you watch television a lot?"

It was Jeanne's turn to make conversation. He had played his part valiantly, in his own opinion, positively heroically.

Lina kept looking at him when she thought no one was noticing. As soon as he turned toward her, she went pink, as if he had caught her in the act of doing something guilty. What was it that made her feel guilty?

She had slim legs and childishly bony knees. Her bare arms were childishly thin, too. Her small, regular teeth were very white.

"The market women must wonder why you follow me

every morning. Do you hear, Franz? Monsieur Virieu goes out at the same time as me, and we walk the same way for nearly two hundred yards. It won't be long before they'll be saying he's in love with me."

Her husband burst out laughing.

"What a marvelous idea!" he exclaimed.

Jeanne was visibly surprised.

They were joking, but it was no joking matter to Emile. He endeavored to smile but could only manage to make a wry grimace. Was she making fun of him? Or was she issuing a kind of challenge to her husband?

They stayed at the Kellers' for nearly an hour. It was Emile who first rose to go.

"I still have a few little things to do before going to bed."

"And we're leaving very early tomorrow morning."

He would not see her coming out of her apartment and going downstairs after flashing a smile at him. He would not follow her along the sidewalk as far as the butcher's or the delicatessen shop.

"Thank you so much for having us and for your excellent cake."

"We hope you'll come again."

Emile held out his hand somewhat hesitantly, knowing how forcefully Keller was going to grip it.

They found themselves back in their own apartment.

"What do you think of them?" Jeanne asked, merely for the sake of saying something, for she sensed that he was in a bad temper.

"They forced me to eat cake."

"It was very good. Perhaps a little too sweet for my taste, but Alsatians do make their cakes very sweet."

He removed his jacket and went to get the dog. Then he sat down in his armchair, put the dog on his knees, and remained there, sitting in stony silence. It was too late to start watching television—they had missed the last program anyway—and too early to go to bed.

Jeanne went into the bathroom to change into a dressing gown.

"It's strange," she remarked when she returned. "As I told them, I've lived in this house for twenty-five years, and I'd never set foot in the apartment opposite ours. It was quite some time after I first came before I even caught a glimpse of the people who lived there. You're not angry with me?"

"What about?"

"For having almost said yes when she came to invite us. She seemed to want us so much to come."

"I wonder why."

"Perhaps out of mere curiosity. Or else, since she's alone for most of the week, she gets bored. It's an odd life for a young bride. They're both so bright and cheerful. One feels they have no neuroses or complexes."

He mumbled "Yes" vaguely, but he was not too sure that he agreed. Perhaps it was true of François Keller. But was it true of Lina?

He knew her name now, and in some ways he could form a clearer idea of her. Yet she still mystified him.

He forced himself to read a few pages of a book about life in Paris during the Revolution. Then, when it was ten o'clock, he got up from his chair.

"Let's go to bed."

It was always he who gave the signal. Jeanne would not have allowed herself to do so. He carried the dog into the bedroom on its cushion.

A quarter of an hour later, he was in his bed and the room was dark.

"Good night, Emile."

"Good night, Jeanne."

It took him quite a while to get to sleep. He lay for a long time in that state of somnolence, in which one can no longer consciously control one's thoughts or imagination.

What had struck him most forcibly that day was neither his visit to the Kellers nor Lina's curious glances but the coffin carried by the four undertaker's men. The sight of it had suddenly made him aware of death, not as an abstract idea, but as a concrete fact.

He was not afraid of dying. All that he wished was that his last illness would be as short as possible. He imagined himself in bed, unable to get up, with Jeanne looking after him and having to deal with his most intimate needs.

Or else he might become a paralytic in a wheel chair, like that still-young man who sold National Lottery tickets at the corner of the street. He would not have the right to live alone. He would not even be able to put himself to bed.

Who would close his eyes? Jeanne? The doctor? Would they take him to a hospital where other patients, bedridden like himself, would watch him and where every now and then one of them would disappear on a stretcher?

He forced himself to think of Lina and her light blue eyes.

What had happened to him during his life? What would he find to put down on the balance sheet?

Nothing. Almost nothing. A dull, disagreeable childhood during which he had served his apprenticeship to solitude. If the girls who promenaded arm in arm turned around to look at him, they promptly burst out laughing.

It was not their fault. He did not even try to look or behave like other people. He saw the world as if through a magnifying glass, and everything in it appeared menacing.

That had lasted for several years. At night he used to wake up with a start because a giant was sitting on his stomach and chest. It was a dream he had had dozens of times, like the one of the house that had collapsed, leaving him buried under the debris. He could hear the voices of the rescuers, as if they were very close. They were talking in a perfectly natural way.

"Cigarette?"

"Thanks."

"Do you think there are any more stiffs under there?"

"We'd have to know how many people lived in the house and how many of them were at home."

He shouted. He thought he was shouting, but he made no more noise than a fish opening its mouth out of water.

Someone went to get a bottle of wine in a neighboring *bistro*.

"You first, Fred. You've worked the hardest."

"But you're the one who found the woman smashed to a pulp."

He knew that he was dreaming. He knew that dream by heart. He tried to shorten it, for it was agonizing. Dirt was getting into his mouth and nostrils and suffocating him.

This morning, as he had looked at the coffin, he had thought of his brother-in-law, who was lying in that box, no longer able to breathe.

He was only forty-four. The odds were that he would live another twenty, perhaps thirty, years. Who knew that Jeanne would not be the first of them to fall ill?

Women lived to be older than men. That was a known fact. Yet there are exceptions. He would be incapable of looking after her. He had a horror of illness. They would have to get a nurse. He would put a cot in the living room.

He owed no one anything, for no one had ever given him anything for nothing.

But, no, he was wrong. There was that girl Lina who had freely given him her childish smile and her blue-eyed glances.

Why?

She represented everything he had never known. His sister had not had that freshness or that ingenuousness when she was young.

Was it really ingenuousness? Was it not more likely deliberate provocation? There are women, particularly young girls, who feel the need to test their sex appeal on every man they meet.

"What's the matter with you?"

He recognized the voice of Jeanne, who had turned on the bedside lamp.

"Why do you ask me that?"

"You were moaning as if you were in pain."

"I suppose it's that cake."

She made him drink half a glass of water with a teaspoonful of bicarbonate dissolved in it.

"Thank you."

It was not the cake, but his dream. He could not tell her about it. He had never told anyone about it. He had never confided anything to anyone. No one knew what he thought or what he felt. In any case, probably no one would have understood.

He was sufficient unto himself. He prided himself on his independence. Jeanne had been a concession, above all a concession to the practical demands of life. He no longer had to eat in restaurants. The apartment was more pleasant than a hotel room. She woke him up when she heard him moaning. She had taken excellent care of him one winter when he had had influenza.

And now they even had a dog!

He had been surprised to see how much his father had aged. His mother had put on weight, lost most of her hair, and acquired a double chin, but that did not worry him.

He had never seen his father ill. Never, to his knowledge, had he once missed a night's baking.

The last time he had seen him, his complexion had been an ugly greyish yellow, and his skin hung loose where the flesh had wasted away. Some obscure disease that had not yet openly manifested itself must have begun to undermine him.

Perhaps there would soon be a second funeral in the family.

Lina was going away with her husband for the weekend. She represented something, he did not know exactly what. His father represented nearly sixty years of hard work (for he had been apprenticed at fourteen) and more or less imminent death.

Emile was no longer afraid. By now he was fast asleep.

Chapter VI

ON Saturday morning, when he emerged from his apartment, he looked at the door across the way, knowing there was no one behind it. He had been eating his boiled eggs when he heard the Kellers go downstairs. Then there had been the sound of a car starting up. He might have gone to the window to watch them leave, but he did not dare to because of Jeanne.

Would he have done so, even if Jeanne had not been there? He could not be sure. He preferred not to know exactly what he felt about Lina. What he did know for certain was that he was not in love with her.

He worked in his cage until midday. For some reason, he could not concentrate as usual. At moments he had to rouse himself from a kind of torpor that he could not account for. Was he not unconsciously putting himself into that state so as to give free rein to his thoughts?

He did not work on Saturday afternoons. He nearly suggested to his wife that they go to the movies. He felt alone, suspended in the void.

During lunch he changed his mind. Having finished his meal, he put on his hat.

"Are you going for a walk?"

"Yes."

He gave a passing glance at that diabolical door, which was destroying his peace of mind, insofar as he had ever had any. He liked strolling through the streets without having Jeanne at his elbow. He could let his thoughts roam freely while continuing to look at passers-by and window displays. This afternoon, as always, his steps instinctively led him toward the Seine.

He walked slowly, stopping every now and then to stare at something, no matter what, a newspaper kiosk, a little boy who was crying, a woman pushing a baby carriage.

What had suddenly come over him at forty-four? She was half his age. She had only just married a tall, robust husband with an open face and a naturally cheerful expression.

This had nothing in common with what had happened to Fernand. It was neither love nor sexual passion. He had no desire to sleep with her, not even to kiss her.

It was something much more complex and disquieting. He had recently had another of his recurring dreams, including the one of the mountains.

He was alone in a rowboat. He had removed his jacket and tie, undone his shirt collar and rolled up his sleeves, things he never did. He was rowing on a great lake, whose calm surface reflected the faintest cloud as clearly as a mirror.

It was very hot. The sun was shining, but, strangely, it was an almost black sun.

The lake was surrounded by mountains entirely covered

with dark green fir trees. He could see no valley between them nor any outlet to the lake. He was not trying to find one. He was simply rowing.

For some unknown reason he had to cross the lake, but every time he looked back to see how far he had gone he saw that he had made no progress at all.

He had had that dream only three times in his life. The first time had been when he was twelve and had been in bed with measles.

He was seized with a sudden, fearful apprehension and broke into a cold sweat. He resisted, but without knowing or wanting to know what he resisted. It was a secret that he dared not reveal to himself.

The following Monday Franz Keller drove off in the open car after waving up from down below to the window where his wife was obviously watching him.

When Emile opened his door at half-past eight, she had opened hers and called out gaily:

"Good morning!"

"Good morning."

He made her go downstairs ahead of him. They lived on the second floor and seldom took the elevator, which was old and alarmingly jerky.

"Did you have a nice Sunday?"

"We went for a walk."

"You and your wife?"

"Yes."

"Do you talk much, the two of you?"

"No, not much."

As they edged their way through the crowd of housewives, she gave passing glances at the fruit and vegetables piled on the barrows of the sidewalk vendors.

"Have you any men friends?"

"No."

"Don't you need them?"

"I suppose not."

"You haven't known many women, have you?"

She was gay, spontaneous. She said all this playfully, with an air of improvisation.

"I've known very few."

"Do you have a sister?"

They were now in front of the butcher's, and they stood there on the sidewalk to continue their talk.

"Yes, I have one. When we were children, at Etampes, I never paid any attention to her."

"And not to her friends, either?"

"That's right. I was frightened of girls."

"Frightened of what?"

"I always had the feeling that they were making fun of me. I went to Paris. Then, a year later, my sister came, too. We lived in different neighborhoods. We each had our own interests. She's a widow now. Her husband committed suicide last week. . . ."

"Was he neurotic?"

"He was in love with another woman."

"You won't mind, will you, if I tell you the first impression you made on me? I took you for a widower, or an unfrocked priest. Does that annoy you?"

"No."

"Now it's time I started my marketing. See you tomorrow."

It was as if she were deliberately making an appointment with him.

There were moments when she irritated him, but that did not make him look forward any less impatiently to half past eight next morning.

When, in spite of himself, he attempted to analyze his own feelings, he decided that he was not unhappy. He was not happy either. His mind spun round and round in emptiness like a disengaged gear wheel. It had never done anything else, and it made him giddy.

A word came back to him from the depths of his childhood when he was learning the catechism: limbo. Limbo, where souls who deserved neither heaven nor hell were bored to death throughout eternity.

He, too, lived in limbo. Perhaps that was why people stared at him curiously. He was different. He belonged to another world.

Jeanne had always observed him closely, as if to protect him from himself. Ever since they had acquired their new neighbors, she had given him a furtive glance as soon as he arrived home and bent down over the dog as it jumped up at him.

"Are you tired?"

"No."

He loathed that question, which his mother was always asking him when he was a child. Why should he be tired?

"I feel perfectly well."

He suffered from nothing except his periodic headaches, to which he had long been inured.

The days went by. Irrationally, he counted them. Six days. Seven days. Eight days after Lina, as one says so many centuries after Jesus Christ.

It was only in his glass cage, correcting the newly printed proofs which blackened his fingers, that he knew any peace.

What was he afraid of? He was increasingly aware of a vague, indefinable anxiety, and he constantly found himself re-envisaging his brother-in-law's coffin. And yet he was not frightened of death.

So what was it he feared?

One afternoon his sister called him up.

"Are you all right, Emile?"

Was it not rather he who should have asked her that question?

"Good news! I've found a job in a boutique in Rue du Faubourg Saint-Honoré. It's a very smart shop that sells only expensive things and caters to the carriage trade."

"Have you started working?"

"No. I'm not starting till the first of September, since I still have so much to do. I have to see the lawyer and the insurance people again and if possible find a cheaper apartment. For the children's sake, I don't want to have to move out to one of those high-rise buildings in the suburbs."

He could not bring himself to take any interest in what she was telling him. However, since he was expected to make some comment, he mumbled:

"That's all very good. I'm glad for your sake."

Every morning they walked side by side, he and Lina, and she was always gay and provocative. One could have sworn that she was trying to seduce him. Wasn't she behaving like those young girls who lead a man on, then suddenly burst out laughing, put out their tongues and run away?

On Friday night, Franz Keller returned from his sales trip, and as Emile passed their front door he heard them talking in Alsatian dialect. Naturally, he could not understand what they were saying.

On Saturday, after lunch, Jeanne asked him:

"Are you going out?"

"Yes."

He had an object in view. He needed his afternoon to go where he had suddenly decided to go.

He made his way to Rue Dareau, where Doctor Thévenin lived. He had treated him some years previously for a severe attack of boils. His arms and chest had been covered with them, and Jeanne had had to make him hot linseed poultices.

There were five people in the waiting room, only one of whom was reading one of the magazines strewn on the table. The others were staring into space, thinking God knows what thoughts.

Every time they heard the footsteps of the nurse approaching the frosted-glass door, there was a rustle of movement, and people tentatively started to rise from their seats. Then the nurse would enter and announce a name.

"Madame Boussac."

This was a fat woman who must still be wearing whalebone corsets. In doctors' waiting rooms one meets types of human beings one never sees anywhere else.

There were two men. One of them had a tic and kept putting his hand up to his nose as if he were brushing off an invisible fly. The other seemed anxious, and he got up two or three times to go over to the window.

Emile waited for an hour and a half, and by the time the nurse came to summon him he no longer knew for certain what he had come for.

To be reassured? But how could Doctor Thévenin, who hardly knew him, reassure him?

He was about sixty and had a square pepper-and-salt beard.

"I've treated you before, haven't I?"

"Yes. For boils."

"Just tell me your name again, will you?"

"Emile Virieu."

He consulted a file and drew out a card with several lines written on it. Emile would have liked to know what notes the doctor had made on him, but here in his consulting room he seemed remote and impersonal.

"Sit down. What is it you're complaining of?"

"Nothing definite."

"You suffer from indigestion? You have bilious attacks, headaches?"

"Headaches, yes. Ever since I was a child."

"Where exactly?"

He indicated the base of his skull.

"Do you have them often?"

"Sometimes every week, sometimes every month."

"Do they last long?"

"A few days. The pain killer a doctor prescribed for me some time ago has no effect on me. I've got used to it."

"Did you have any of the usual childhood illnesses?"

"Only measles."

For once he would have liked to talk, but the doctor's look intimidated him.

"Sometimes I have sudden fits of trembling, or I break out in a sweat."

"Are you married?"

"Yes."

"Do you get on well with your wife?"

"We never quarrel."

"Do you love her?"

"No."

"Why did you marry her?"

"Perhaps not to be alone any more."

"How long have you been married?"

"Nearly twenty years."

"Does *she* love *you*?"

"I don't think so. She looks after me well. She doesn't try to influence me in any way."

"Does she work?"

"She translates English and American books, which means she can stay at home all day. She goes out only to do her shopping."

"Do you hate her?"

Emile had been looking the doctor straight in the face, as if to defy him, and now and then there had been a faint smile on Thévenin's lips.

"I don't think so."

"You're not really sure?"

"There are moments when I hate the whole world."

"Why?"

"Because. . ."

He did not go on with his sentence.

"Because what?"

He muttered almost inaudibly:

"Because I'm not like them."

"What difference is there between you and other people?"

"I don't know."

"Are you jealous?"

"No."

"Is your wife unfaithful to you?"

"I should be surprised if she were, for she'd have difficulty in finding a lover."

The doctor did not press him further.

"Let's go into the other room."

It was a small room, in the middle of which was an examination table covered in green plastic.

"Get undressed. You'll find a coat hanger over there."

The doctor returned to his consulting room. Emile undressed reluctantly. He kept on his underpants and socks. He waited, standing up, for the doctor to reappear, which he did not do for some time.

"Lie down and try to relax."

The doctor prodded various spots in his abdomen, then in the region of his liver.

"Sit up."

He tested his reflexes by tapping his knees with a little nickel-plated hammer; then he ran some pointed object over the soles of his feet.

"Is everything normal?"

"Stay sitting up."

He ran a stethoscope over his back and chest.

"Take a deep breath."

The doctor stood up. Emile tried to make for his clothes.

"Not yet. Come in here.

He was taken into another equally small room and made to stand up close against an X-ray screen.

"Turn slightly to one side. Keep absolutely still."

The room went dark except for a very dim glow, like a faint mist, which came from nowhere.

"Take a deep breath."

He wished he had not come. He no longer felt like a man. He was being treated as if he were a guinea pig.

"Now turn and face me. Breathe in. Hold your breath."

The light came on again.

"Your lungs are excellent. So is your heart."

They returned to the next room.

"Sit down again for a moment on the edge of the table."

He felt his skull as if he were trying to dig his fingers into it.

"Am I hurting you?"

"No."

"Am I now?"

"A little."

"Is that what you feel when you have your headaches?"

"No."

"You may get dressed again."

The doctor returned to his consulting room. When he was ready, Emile knocked on the door.

"Come in."

He was making notes on his card in very small, very fine writing.

"You've never consulted a neurologist?"

"No."

"Perhaps you ought to. I think your aches and pains are symptoms of some nervous rather than physical disorder. Do you know of one?"

"No."

"I'm going to give you the name and address of an excellent colleague of mine—Doctor Férenczi, who lives on Avenue du Maine. He has a clinic at Saint-Anne's. You'll have to ask his secretary for an appointment."

The doctor wrote the name and address on a sheet of his prescription pad. He rose to his feet. The consultation was over.

"How much do I owe you?"

"Do you have medical insurance?"

"No."

"That will be fifty francs."

When he was back on the street, he felt vexed. He would have liked the doctor to find something definite the matter with him, some organic disease that could have been treated with pills or a diet.

Why was he trying to send him to a neurologist? Wasn't that almost the same thing as a psychiatrist?

He had no intention of going to see Doctor Férenczi. Certainly he knew he was not like other people, but he was sure that he was not suffering from any mental illness.

He had wasted his afternoon. He was neither more

reassured nor more alarmed after being examined by the bearded doctor. He broke out into one of those sweats that were recurring more and more frequently and which had not escaped his wife's watchful eye.

He went into a *bistro*, something he seldom did, and ordered a glass of beer at the zinc counter.

Why did this doctor, too, like the one at Nevers, want him to see a neurologist, he asked himself once again. Did they both suspect him of being abnormal?

He was not exactly like other men, granted. He had known that for a long time.

He had made love to Jeanne only for a few weeks after their marriage, and since then they had had no physical contact. In eighteen years he had six times at the most stopped a prostitute in the street and followed her into some malodorous little hotel.

He emerged from the bar and went on walking. He thought of Lina. It was true that he did not want to make love to her. It was not her body, with its unfinished look, that attracted him. She did not look like a woman but like a very young girl, hardly more than a child. Her behavior, this game she was playing with him, was just as childish.

Nevertheless, she was immensely important to him. Why? He searched painfully for an answer to this question, but he could not find one.

At a street corner on Boulevard Saint-Michel, a woman with large breasts smiled at him invitingly.

"Want to come, dearie?"

He hesitated. Then, mechanically, he followed her down a side street.

"You'll see. . . . I'll be ever so nice to you."

She would have done better to keep quiet. He had not the least desire to hear her talk. He did not even have any desire to go to bed with her.

"Got something on your mind?" asked the woman, whose face he could see within a few inches of his own.

"No."

"Are you always so nervous? If you don't calm down, you may not be able to make it."

"I don't care."

It was not true. He was humiliated by his failure, and he would have liked to hit her to punish her. He suddenly hated her as he hated the rest of the world.

"What are you doing?"

"Getting dressed."

"You're not going to go off without paying me?"

He threw a fifty-franc note on the bed, opened the door, and slunk along the passage and down the stairs as if he had something shameful to hide.

The sky was becoming overcast after a cloudless week. His skin was damp and sticky. He hoped there would be a thunderstorm; it might deliver him from the weight he felt pressing down on his shoulders.

When he got back to the apartment on Rue du Faubourg-Saint-Jacques, Jeanne, who was sitting by the open window with the dog on her lap, looked at him inquiringly.

Strangely enough, she used the same words as the prostitute.

"Have you something on your mind?"

She spoke in her usual quiet, humble way, and she was surprised at his reaction.

"No. I've nothing on my mind. And if there's one thing I loathe, it's being asked idiotic questions."

"I'm sorry. I said that just as I might have said anything else."

"You'd have done better to say something else."

"Why are you angry?"

"Because I've had enough of being spied on. I can't so much as frown without your noticing it and asking me questions."

It was the first time he had lost his temper with her. Certainly she knew the expression of his face at all hours of the day and almost of the night. But was it not he who had wanted this? She endeavored in every way to protect him, to anticipate his wishes. It was quite natural for her to be anxious when she felt anything was the matter with him.

Now, once again, it was he who was in the wrong. She had asked him a perfectly ordinary, inoffensive question.

"Sometimes, the way you look at me when I come home, anyone would think you were jealous."

"Nevertheless, I'm not, and you know it. In any case, I wouldn't have the right to be."

"What makes you stay with me? Can you tell me that?"

"You're my friend, aren't you?"

"That's enough for you?"

"Yes."

He was annoyed with her for making him have to think, as if he did not think far too much already. He now began to wonder what the root cause of his unwonted irritability was and whether it did not date back to the drama of Fernand Lamark.

He had just spoken as vehemently as his brother-in-law had done. Once again he envisaged Fernand, excited by drink, in the *brasserie* on Boulevard Montparnasse, talking so loudly that the proprietor had come over and asked him to lower his voice. Just now, he himself had almost shouted. So nearly so that the dog on Jeanne's lap had trembled all over and looked at him with obvious anxiety.

"Don't pay any attention. I expect it's the weather. There's thunder in the air, and it always affects me."

"I'm not cross with you. Would you like it if we went out and had dinner in a restaurant?"

"No."

People outside were just as much enemies as those inside.

He envisaged Fernand again as he had been that night when he came to the apartment. His state had worsened. He could hardly stand upright. He had held forth volubly and incoherently, gesticulating all the time, and his blood-shot eyes must have seen everything as distorted.

From that moment he had been a man cast adrift and no doubt already marked down by fate.

What was Emile's fate? What force was driving him on, an unknown force that frightened him?

It had nothing to do with Lina. She was merely a chance incident to which he attached not the slightest importance.

There were some rumblings of thunder a long way off in the direction of Passy. He went to the window to look at the sky and saw heavy clouds scudding across it. The wind began to blow hard, and he had to shut the two windows. Out in the street people walked faster but without escaping the squall.

First, a cloud of dust rushed past like a cyclone; then huge drops of rain splashed the paving stones with black spots. The thunder burst out right overhead, and in a few seconds the rain was coming down in torrents.

The passers-by no longer ran along the sidewalks but took shelter in doorways.

Huge drops lashed violently against the windows. The dog was now curled up in a ball on Jeanne's lap, and she was stroking him to reassure him.

"He's frightened," she murmured.

She was holding out an olive branch to him by talking like this about something else in a natural voice.

He did not answer. No answer was required. He was still thinking of Fernand Lamark and that light oak coffin. One day, when he was feeling calm and clearheaded, he would make his will. In it he would give orders that he was to be cremated, for he did not want to be shut up in a box. Neither did he want people to come and see him on his deathbed or to accompany him into a church and then to the cemetery.

He would like to die without anyone's knowing. He did not want people to talk about him. He did not want them to pity him, only to forget him as soon as they left the house where his corpse lay.

The squalls followed each other in quick succession, for they came in waves, with brief intervals of calm. Swelling streams coursed along the gutters, and the water gurgled noisily down the drains.

He dared not tell his wife that his nerves were so tense that he longed for a glass of brandy or any kind of spirits. Jeanne would have looked at him more anxiously than ever, for ordinarily he did not drink. Besides, it made him think of his brother-in-law.

That death had left its mark on him. He had, so to speak, been present at it. Chance had willed that he should witness all its stages, except for the final gesture.

There were still a few claps of thunder, already much farther away; then suddenly the rain stopped falling, the wind stopped blowing, and one could see the dark shapes of the passers-by emerging from their shelters.

He opened the windows and took deep breaths of the freshened, purified air.

"A thunderstorm always comes as a relief, don't you think?" said Jeanne.

She had to put the dog down, for it was time for her to go and cook the dinner. Emile sat in his armchair to read the paper. He felt a little relaxed.

He was annoyed with himself for having been so furious with Jeanne. After all, his very reason for marrying her had been his need to have the presence of another human being at his side. How, since they lived together, could she not be aware of every detail of his life? After so many years she knew all his foibles and idiosyncrasies and the premonitory signs of his fits of depression.

He thought he could rely on keeping calm for the rest of the day. At half past seven they sat down at the table and, after the soup, had fishcakes.

They watched television, sitting side by side in the semi-darkness, and at a quarter past ten they switched it off.

Jeanne went to turn on the lights. He felt that she had something on her mind and was hesitant about bringing it up. At first, she opened her mouth without saying anything; then she said in a soft voice that was meant to be persuasive:

"Emile, you don't think perhaps you're being indiscreet?"

It was the sequel to the scene that had gone before. Only this time the words were more definite.

Why did he feel the need to act the part of a husband who has no idea what his wife is talking about and stare at her in astonishment? At that moment his heart was full of venom. He was angry with her for everything, for being ugly, for never losing her temper, for always having that indulgent smile, above all for judging him.

For she did judge him, even if she did not let him see it. How did she see him? What did she really know about him?

Was his anger visible in his protruding eyes, whose fixed stare was beginning to embarrass her?

"You know I'm not jealous, and the feelings you may have about her are no concern of mine. But don't forget she has a husband. Even if he's away most of the week, someone might say something to him or even send him an anonymous letter. We've got the reputation of being standoffish because we keep to ourselves. Some of the neighbors may resent it."

It was obvious that she had decided to go through with it to the bitter end and that she considered it her duty to put him on his guard.

"Everyone, the concierge to begin with, sees you go off together every morning."

He was still seething with anger. He said defiantly:

"So what? Does that annoy you?"

"Of course not. But if the husband were told about it or came back sooner than expected. . . ."

"Am I responsible for the time she does her marketing? Am I expected to change the timetable I've kept to for nearly twenty years?"

"I'm only advising you to be careful for your own sake, Emile."

Was it not just the sort of thing his mother would have

said, in the tone of one who knows all the ways of Providence?

There was a silence and Noris yawned. For a moment Emile felt angry with him, too, and could have kicked him.

"You've changed, Emile."

"Everyone changes. Fernand has changed quite remarkably. He's dead."

He was pleased with what he considered a witty remark and added, looking at her sarcastically:

"*You've* changed, too."

It was unnecessarily malicious, and he was vexed with himself for having said it. It was time to go to bed, and he went into the bedroom, then into the bathroom. He looked at himself in the mirror, and his face seemed to him not only ugly but rather frightening.

The painful half-hour, sometimes hour, was about to begin. Once in bed, once the good nights had been exchanged and the bedside lamp switched off, the fear of his nightmares began to haunt him. They were becoming more and more frequent, more and more alarming.

At the beginning his mind was clear, and he nearly always went over the events of the day, as if there was something reassuring about drawing up this daily balance sheet.

Today's was a bad one. He attributed this to various reasons, including the storm, but he knew that none of them was the true one. He knew the real reason for his behavior. That reason was called Férenczi. Doctor Thévenin had examined him thoroughly and found nothing wrong. Or if he had, he had said nothing about it.

Did a doctor have the right to conceal his diagnosis from his patient? Emile knew nothing about medical ethics so he could not answer the question.

The fact remained that Thévenin had advised him to see a neurologist. Was there much difference between a neurologist and a psychiatrist?

Was this advice the inevitable result of the examination that the doctor had carried out and the questionnaire to which he had subjected him? Why, for example, ask him if he loved his wife or if he were jealous? He had asked him other questions that had no apparent connection with his health.

Férenczi had a clinic at Saint-Anne's. Wasn't that one of those establishments where they treated madmen?

He was not mad. Some people could almost make him think he was, the way they looked at him.

He was not like them, granted. He had no need of a specialist to make him aware that he was different. But hadn't one the right to be different? He did not like other men. He was incapable of making contact with them, just as, at school, he had never made any contact with other boys.

"Why don't you go out and play?"

How many times had his mother repeated that eternal refrain? And the other one:

"You've always got your nose stuck in a book. It's no wonder you have to wear glasses."

He had always read voraciously. Anything, no matter what. It was his particular form of escapism. And what about the others—for example, those who went fishing and spent hours staring at a little red cork and making their children keep quiet? And those who spent every evening in the smoky atmosphere of a night club, staring at half-naked women? And those who . . .

Was it not they who were different? So why was he frightened? And of what? He was beginning to be afraid of Jeanne's looks. And he had taken to putting off falling asleep as long as possible, for fear of having a nightmare.

Finally he dozed off, and though he did have a nightmare, it was not a particularly alarming one. There was thunder and lightning, and he was walking bareheaded along a road, singing. In fact, he never sang. He had never sung, even at school, where, at choir practice, he had been content to open his mouth at the right time without emitting a sound.

He woke up tired. This was nothing new. He had always found it difficult to get going in the morning.

"Good morning," he muttered, as he walked through the living room where Jeanne was typing.

"Good morning, Emile."

She discreetly avoided looking at him, and he went into the kitchen to pour himself his first cup of coffee. He drank it slowly. All told, this was one of the best moments of the day, apart from the time he spent in his glass cage.

He shaved and was once more obliged to look at himself and to dislike what he saw. He took his shower. His movements followed each other with such mechanical precision that he knew exactly how long each stage of his toilet took him and had no need to look at the clock.

He ate his boiled eggs, with Jeanne, as usual, sitting opposite him to keep him company.

He felt slightly ashamed of his behavior the day before, but he did not want to admit it in so many words. He contented himself with saying:

"It's going to be hot again."

It was unusual for him to volunteer a remark on the weather, and in his own mind this was as good as an apology. Jeanne took it as such.

"Yes. Last night I had to get up because Noris was whimpering. I wondered if he was ill and went to have a look at him. He was dreaming and twitching his hind legs as if he were trying to run."

"There's no reason why animals shouldn't dream."

It was Sunday. If he got up at the same time as on weekdays, it was from habit. Besides, if he lingered on in bed, he felt out of sorts all the rest of the day.

There was no encounter on the landing that morning, and he had not given any thought to what he was going to do to fill up the time.

"Do you intend to work long?"

"That depends on what you want to do."

"I haven't any plans."

"Aren't you going for a walk?"

He did so nearly every Sunday morning. He liked the empty streets, the dark-clad figures making their way to the churches or emerging from them, the occasional swells of organ music as he passed their open doors.

"There's a very good film at the Champs-Elysées," she ventured to suggest.

"Who directed it?"

"Fellini."

He liked Fellini, but his films frightened him because he too was "different."

"At what time?"

"The first performance is at two. The second at five."

"We'll go to the first. We need only to have an early lunch."

He went on his walk and paced through the streets, feeling as lonely as can be. He did not think. He did not want to think. Once again he visualized the *brasserie* on Boulevard Montparnasse, the Coq d'Or, where his brother-in-law had asked him to meet him. At that moment, had not Fernand had some kind of premonition?

He himself had one. Not today especially. Not merely for the past few days. Ever since he had been born, in fact.

Two children dressed in their Sunday best were walking in front of their parents, also dressed in theirs, and the wife left a scent of flowers in her wake. He would have liked the world to be like this, himself included. Unfortunately, that ideal world did not exist.

Everybody lied. They lied to other people and to themselves. Did not Emile lie to himself too?

His employer, Monsieur Jodet, who had worked so hard and was still doing so, had a selfish, extravagant wife, who ruled him with an iron rod. His son was no better, and he had given up any idea of making him a partner in the firm. This did not prevent him from looking as cheerful as if he were the luckiest man in the world.

Perhaps, at times, he managed to persuade himself that he was?

His own father had been apprenticed at fourteen. He had spent nearly all his nights shut up in the bakery, sleeping only by day, and waking himself up with a bottle of white wine. He practically never saw his son and daughter, and his wife was tied to their shop.

He was always laughing and telling smutty jokes that everyone knew by heart. When he was alone, did he not drop that mask of cheerfulness and give a wry grimace as he thought of the hidden disease that was secretly devouring him and would carry him off one day?

All the tradesmen of the town would come to his funeral. So would all the neighbors and the customers of the bakery.

Where would his wife go? She could not run the business on her own. Nor could she impose herself on either of her two children. In any case, she had a horror of Paris, where she never felt safe.

She would rent a little one-room apartment with a kitchen and perhaps a bathroom. Or else she would go into a home for old ladies.

Did she ever think about it? He, Emile, faced up to reality. Yet it was not even reality. It was interwoven with his dreams and fantasies. He led a double life.

On one side, there was the glass cage, where no one ever thought of disturbing him. On the other was all the rest. And the rest included passers-by, old men, cripples, children, all the people one happens to meet daily in a big city, not to mention Jeanne and Lina.

Lina was something apart. He was still not sure what he felt about her. His opinion of her varied from hour to hour, but that did not make him look forward any the less to meeting her every morning on the landing.

While he and Jeanne were having lunch, they listened to the news on the radio. He was not interested in it, but it took the place of conversation.

Jeanne dressed herself with more care than on weekdays, like the women he had seen going to Mass. And she, too, put a little scent on the collar of her dress.

They took the métro and had to change at Châtelet, where a flood of human beings was streaming through the endless subterranean passages.

Outside the movie house there was a queue fifty yards long, and they took their places at the end of it.

The people's faces wore an expression of patient resignation. They were here for pleasure, for the two and a half hours they were going to spend in front of the screen.

Other men and women, singly or in couples, joined the queue and waited behind them. At intervals the whole line took a step or two forward.

Finally, they reached the chain, which was withdrawn to let in six people at a time.

"Two seats, please."

"Balcony. I've only twelve-franc balcony seats left."

He paid.

Then, with his wife at his side, he took his seat in the darkened auditorium.

Chapter VII

IT WAS a grey, muggy morning, close and oppressive. At half past eight she was there to meet him on the landing. Instead of pants and a jumper, she was wearing a skin-tight dress of fine red jersey.

The women with the fruit and vegetable barrows were out in full force and shouting their wares to attract the passers-by. Most of them had ruddy faces and loud voices and kept up a running exchange of ribald jokes.

One of them called out to her neighbor, loud enough for the others to hear:

"Just look at that handsome couple! If they have kids, I'll ask them to keep one for me."

Emile turned pale. He wondered if Lina had heard. The next moment she asked him in her high-pitched childish voice:

"Aren't you afraid of falling in love with me?"

"No."

He said it so emphatically that she was momentarily taken aback.

"Don't you think I'm pretty?"

"I suppose you are. I'm no expert."

"It's because I'm too young, isn't it? Yet I've always heard that older men prefer very young girls. Anyway, I'm not all that young. I'm twenty."

Around some of the little barrows there was a positive swarm of housewives, and the chatter of voices made a constant hum all along the street.

"You're on the landing at the same time every morning."

"For eighteen years I've been leaving my apartment at half past eight to go to the printer's."

"Didn't you miss seeing me on Saturday?"

He preferred not to answer, but his brow darkened.

"Doesn't your wife ever go out?"

"She does her marketing every morning, like you. Only she does it a little later."

"Doesn't she ever go out in the afternoon to do some shopping in the center of town?"

"On Wednesdays she does. She goes to take the chapters she's translated to her publisher, on the right bank. She uses the opportunity to buy anything special she needs and can't get nearby."

"She isn't jealous?"

"No."

"Franz would be furiously jealous if he had any reason to be. To look at him, you'd think he was an easygoing man, always smiling and good-tempered and as meek as a lamb. But he can fly into terrible rages, and he's tremendously strong."

"Are you afraid of him?"

"It's fun to feel a bit afraid. When I was much younger and still living in our village—it's no more than a crossroads, really—I used to go out in the dark on purpose. I used to hum to keep up my courage. My parents used to get anxious and come and look for me. Yet it wasn't that I didn't know the risks I was running. I'd read stories in the papers about little girls who'd been attacked and raped and murdered."

They had reached the butcher's.

"Can you understand a man doing that?"

"No."

"Would *you* be capable of doing it?"

"I don't think so."

"You don't seem all that sure."

He did not reply. She looked him straight in the face with her lavender-blue eyes that seemed to be challenging him.

"Till tomorrow."

"Till tomorrow."

He was annoyed and at the same time overexcited. It was as if she were bent on disturbing him, on upsetting what little equilibrium he had. It was a relief to get back to his glass cage, where he became another man.

About ten, the telephone rang. It was Geraldine.

"I'm ashamed to bother you again with my problems. But remember that I'm left alone, that my children no longer have a father. They won't listen to *me*. I've no authority whatever over them."

"What's the trouble?"

"Patrick's got the crazy idea of giving up his studies and going off, no matter how, to the United States or Canada."

"What does he propose to do there?"

"According to him, he'll do anything, no matter what, provided he gets away from here. I've tried to make him change his mind, but I haven't succeeded. You wouldn't see him, would you, Emile?"

"Do you think I'd have any better success than you? He and I hardly know each other. When I go to see you, he's always out."

"Nevertheless, you're a man."

Luckily, she could not see his ironical smile. However, he could not admit to her that he already had enough, and more than enough, problems of his own to cope with.

"When would you like me to see him?"

"As soon as possible. He's already stopped going to his lectures. He spends his time wandering about the Latin Quarter with his own particular bunch of friends. I'm afraid they may be taking drugs. I've been through his pockets when he was asleep and found nothing, but that's no proof. When could he go to see you?"

"Tonight, about half past eight."

"I hope I can persuade him to go. By the way, it would be better if Jeanne weren't in the room. He wouldn't talk so frankly in front of a woman, especially about such personal matters. How is Jeanne? I forgot to ask."

"Very well."

"I also forgot to tell you that I've found a smaller and cheaper apartment on Rue Notre-Dame-de-Lorette, near Place Saint-Georges. It's not much of a place, but it's just been redecorated. The woman who had it before was a barmaid, but she's just signed a long contract for a job in Lebanon."

"I'll telephone you to tell you how things went after I've seen your son."

He was being asked to play a part for which he was not prepared, but he could not refuse.

At dinner that night Jeanne made no allusion to their conversation of two days ago. She must have seen him and Lina from the window. They had stood still, talking longer than usual.

"Patrick may be coming in tonight, at about half past eight," he announced.

Jeanne looked surprised.

"He wants to go to America. His mother's asked me to persuade him not to. I'll do my utmost, but I haven't much hope. It would be better if you weren't in the living room. Your being here might make him nervous."

"I understand. I'll stay in the bedroom."

Patrick arrived a quarter of an hour late. His expression was at once defiant and suspicious.

"My mother told me you wanted to see me."

"Yes. I wanted to have a talk with you. Sit down."

Patrick had quite long hair and wore a turtle-neck sweater, in spite of its being summer.

He heaved a sigh and slumped down in Jeanne's armchair.

"I hear you want to leave home and go abroad. Is this true?"

"Perfectly true. Do you see anything wrong in it?"

"It depends on what you mean to do."

"In other words, if I got my hair cut, put on a shirt and a tie, and got a respectable nine-to-five white-collar job in an office, my mother's mind would be set at rest."

"How old are you?"

"I'll be twenty-one in three months. Then I'll be of age and can do as I like."

"Have you any money?"

"I haven't. My parents didn't give me much. But my friend, who's going with me, has some."

"Where did he get it from?"

"His father's a big industrialist and gives him everything he asks for. We need only our passage money and enough to live on for a month or two. Long enough to get on our feet."

"You think you'll be happier in America?"

"Certainly happier than here."

"Why?"

"First of all, because I shan't be obliged to live with my mother and sister. I'm fed to the teeth with both of them."

"You've only just lost your father, and you're proposing to desert your family."

"He was proposing to desert it, too, when he died, wasn't he?"

"Do you think you'll manage to earn your living over there?"

"One can earn one's living anywhere. It depends on what one is prepared to do."

"And what would you be prepared to do?"

"Anything, no matter what."

He gave his uncle another defiant look.

"Now go ahead with your moral lecture. I'm listening."

"I'm not going to give you a lecture. I shan't try to dissuade you."

"Good God! I seem to have got you all wrong. I always thought of you as hopelessly bourgeois and one mass of complexes and inhibitions."

"Maybe I am hopelessly bourgeois, and maybe I do indeed have complexes and inhibitions. That doesn't prevent me from realizing that other people are different."

"In that case, there's nothing more to discuss. My friend and I leave next week, as soon as we've got our visas."

"But what about your military service?"

"As a student, I've been granted a deferment. If I don't come back when it expires, that's their worry."

He could not doubt that his uncle, whose eyes never left his face, envied him.

Emile, too, at nineteen, had left Etampes and the family bakery to come to Paris. Only he had not had this freedom of spirit. An invisible thread continued to bind him to the world he had left behind.

"You're a good guy. Uncle Emile."

"I knew it was useless to try to stop you."

"You couldn't be more right."

Emile felt a pang of envy. Patrick wanted to escape from the conventional life he led at home. He was going off to seek adventure. Perhaps he would not find it, but at least he would have tried.

"Tell me honestly. Do you take drugs or not?"

"I've tried pot two or three times. I didn't get any kick out of it, so I dropped it."

"And your friend?"

There was an embarrassed silence.

"He smokes hash."

"Much?"

"No. Two or three times a week."

"Does his father know?"

"His father has a mistress, a gorgeous piece, and he lives in an entirely different world from his son's. They meet only by chance. May I go now? He's waiting for me out in the street, and we're throwing a surprise party."

"Yes, you may go."

"Thanks."

Patrick was taller than he and had broader shoulders. He held out his hand and gave his uncle's a hearty shake.

"I guess you're going to call up my mother."

"Yes."

"Tell her, above all, not to waste her energy lecturing me on my morals. I have a horror of scenes."

For a moment Emile stood listening to the sound of his footsteps running downstairs. Then, as it died away, he went into the bedroom to release his wife, who was playing with Noris. The little dog growled, because he was disturbing them.

"Has he gone?"

"Yes."

"Did you succeed?"

"I didn't try. He's a boy who knows what he wants, and you can't make him change his mind."

He dialed his sister's number.

"Well? How did it go?"

"All right."

"He's given up the idea?"

"No. Nothing will make him give it up."

"How on earth does he think he's going to manage out there without any money?"

"He's going with a friend who has a little."

"Don't you think it's madness?"

"No. Wasn't it just as much madness for you to come

to Paris alone without knowing how you were going to earn a living?"

"That's not the same thing."

"Why?"

"Paris is not New York. What's the good of arguing with you? You're obviously completely on Patrick's side."

"Yes. And if you'll take my advice, give up trying to stop him. It's useless, and it'll only turn him against you."

She gave a loud sigh.

"Oh, well. Thanks all the same. Good night, Emile."

Jeanne had no need of explanations. What she had heard was sufficient.

In bed, he thought for a long time about his nephew who had the courage to carry his ideas to the limit. He, Emile, had been obliged to marry Jeanne to bolster up what little self-confidence he possessed.

It was true that he was not as strong and healthy as Patrick.

He had difficulty in getting to sleep. He could not get his conversation of that morning with Lina out of his mind. She was making fun of him. She was playing with fire. Did she imagine that there was no real danger?

In his half-sleep her face dissolved into a blur and became an anonymous face, which might have been that of any girl of her age. He felt frightened, and at the same time impatient.

He tossed and turned in his bed, his whole body in a sweat. He suspected that Jeanne was awake too.

His witness! The witness he himself had chosen because he was incapable of living alone.

Of what *was* he capable? Of nothing, except correcting printer's proofs in his glass-walled cage.

And also, when he walked in the street, of attracting the curiosity of passers-by by his protruding eyes and his fixed stare.

"I'll kill them," he often said to himself automatically, without thinking exactly what the words meant.

Ever since he was a boy they had kept compulsively recurring in his mind like a tune one cannot get out of one's head. Once, not long ago, he had found himself muttering them aloud in the street and actually clenching his fists. He tried to remember when and where. Yes, it was when he had been walking home after his meeting with Fernand at the Coq d'Or. And what he had muttered aloud was not "I'll kill them" but "I'll kill her." He had meant Jeanne.

At last he fell asleep. Contrary to his expectation, he did not dream or, if he did, he did not remember his dream when he woke up.

Jeanne was typing away as usual in the living room, and they exchanged their usual "Good morning" as he went into the kitchen to get his cup of coffee.

Chapter VIII

THERE was a mist and the sky was clouded over, but it was no cooler.

"So tomorrow, then?"

"Tomorrow, what?"

He pretended he had not understood.

"It's Wednesday."

"What difference does its being Wednesday make to anything?"

"Your wife will be out."

"What do you want me to do?"

His throat had gone dry. What was happening this morning did not surprise him. Lina's words were only the climax of something that had begun long ago in the distant past.

"Would you rather come to my apartment, or shall I go to yours?"

He heard himself answer in a hoarse voice:

"I'd rather go to yours."

"What time?"

"About three. My wife usually leaves at half past two."

He was in a hurry to get away from her, to put an end to this embarrassing conversation.

"You're a bit alarmed at the prospect, aren't you?"

"I don't know."

"Is it the first time you've ever done such a thing?"

"Yes."

"The first time in your whole life?"

"Yes."

She smiled, enraptured and excited. This time, outside the butcher's, she held out her hand to him.

"Till tomorrow."

He had a headache all day, and the pills Thévenin had prescribed for him had not the slightest effect. He worked diligently, but every now and then he was obliged to stop and go back on his tracks, for he found he had read through a whole passage without taking in its meaning.

Thévenin had advised him to go and see a nerve specialist, Doctor Férenczi.

What could the nerve specialist do for a case like his?

Contrary to what had happened yesterday, the mist did not lift all day, and there was only an occasional gleam of sunlight.

He found it difficult to breathe. He could hardly wait for tomorrow afternoon.

When he went home to lunch, he looked long and hard at Jeanne as if he were seeing her for the first time, and he understood why the people to whom he had introduced her at the time of their marriage had been so surprised. There are some kinds of ugliness that are amusing and attractive. Hers had something depressing about it.

He wondered, in spite of himself, what she was like

inside, what went on in the brain behind that pasty, ill-featured face.

The evening seemed much longer than usual in coming to an end. He did not want to watch television, but he did so in order that nothing should be different from other days.

He did not even know what the pictures that passed before his eyes represented.

He might have settled on Jeanne. He had thought of doing so many times during the years of their marriage. He had no personal grudge against her. She behaved as discreetly as possible and was intensely concerned about his comfort and health, if not about the happiness she was incapable of giving him.

What happiness? Did such a thing exist? People pretended it did. Nearly everyone pretended it did. She, too, must suffer from her ugliness. As a little girl she had been the laughingstock of her classmates. When she was older, young men must never have asked her to dance with them.

She asked him, in the semidarkness:

"What's the matter with you?"

"Headache."

"Have you taken your pills?"

"Yes."

"You ought to go and see a specialist."

She was talking like Thévenin.

"What sort of specialist?"

"I don't know. There must be someone, somewhere, who could do you some good."

They went to bed at half past ten. He felt exhausted. It seemed to him that his whole body was one vast sensitive sore.

He would tell Monsieur Jodet that he had an appointment with his dentist, though he hardly need bother to find an excuse. He was one of the firm's oldest employees, and no one else was involved in his work.

"O, God, grant that . . ."

He had not believed in God since he was fifteen, but nonetheless he found himself praying desperately:

"Grant that it may not happen."

He felt so utterly miserable. He had felt so all his life. Men lived in society, and he was tacitly excluded from it. It was not imagination on his part. He had only to look at them when he met them in the street.

He could not go out toward them either. Between him and the rest of the world there was an invisible, impassable barrier.

"I'll kill them. . . ."

Sometimes, waves of hatred surged up in his breast. And it was true, at such moments, that he would have killed them all, if he had had the means to.

At other times, it was himself that he detested most. He hated himself for his flabby face, his pallid body, his hesitant movements, his way of hugging the wall when he walked in the street.

What had Lina told him about her husband? That he was strong and . . . He had forgotten the second word, but it was obvious that she admired him.

In the morning, she was there on the landing. She smiled at him, with a little glint in her eyes.

"Slept well?"

"No."

"Because of me?"

"You and all the rest."

"The rest of what?"

"The rest of the world."

"Don't you like the world as it is? *I* think life's marvelous."

She gazed at the barrows with their piles of fruit and vegetables and the bustling crowd on the sidewalk as if she wanted to drink in all the color and life of the street scene.

"I mustn't . . ." he muttered.

He did not realize he was thinking aloud, but his lips had moved and she noticed it.

"What did you say?"

"Nothing. I was talking to myself."

"That doesn't surprise me."

"Why?"

"Because you look the sort of person who talks to himself."

He gripped her wrists. It was as if an obscure power were driving him to throw caution to the winds.

"Three o'clock?"

"Yes."

"You needn't knock. I'll be waiting behind the door to let you in."

How did he manage to work? He did so mechanically. He mentioned his dentist's appointment to Monsieur Jodet.

"I hope he won't hurt you too much."

Was he being ironical?

Emile worked in his cage till noon, and as soon as he was out in the street he was back among his enemies. Men. All men. A world that had never taken him to its bosom.

The cripple who sold lottery tickets was at his street corner in his wheel chair. His head bent down onto his shoulder, and one of his arms was shorter than the other.

"I've cooked you some lamb cutlets."

He could not care less what she had provided for lunch. He had no appetite for food, but he forced himself to eat it. All through the meal, he kept giving little glances at his wife.

Why not her?

He was still hesitating after she had brought in the second course. What finally decided him was that she was stronger than he was.

"Are you going out?"

"Yes, as I always do on Wednesdays. I've finished three chapters, and the publisher will be pleased. He wants to get the book out for Christmas."

Christmas! A fir tree! Little electric lights! Fragile multicolored balls hanging from the branches. Even a Christmas tree was another of their lying contraptions to foster the illusion that there was such a thing as happiness.

He left home at half past one and went and sat in the *brasserie* where he had had his meeting with Fernand— the Coq d'Or on Boulevard Montparnasse. This had no significance. He had nearly an hour to wait. He was incapable of reading the paper. He looked at the people round him and suddenly imagined them in the form of animals.

He had ordered a glass of beer. He never drank anything stronger. He remembered his brother-in-law's overexcitement, which the manager of the *brasserie* had had to try to calm.

He himself was calm. He could not remember ever having been so calm. It was almost serenity. He felt as if he had been delivered of some great burden.

Half past two. Jeanne would be leaving the house, carrying the brief case containing her translation. She was going to take the métro.

He waited another ten minutes, then made his way back to Rue du Faubourg-Saint-Jacques.

She started when she saw him in the frame of the doorway. Perhaps there was fear in her posture. She drew back as he closed the door behind him.

"What are you hoping for?" she asked, once they were in the living room. She was wearing the same red dress she had worn that morning.

"I'm hoping for nothing."

"You realized it was a joke, didn't you?"

There was no mirror in which he could have seen himself. His features were literally rigid, and his face no longer had any expression. He seemed unable to control his movements and might have been taken for a sleepwalker.

"Well, then, why did you come?"

She made an attempt to slip past him and get to the door. He stood there, solidly barring her way, with his arms slightly outstretched.

"What's the matter with you?"

She was going to scream. She opened her mouth, but he had already gripped her throat with both hands.

He saw her eyes, crazy with terror, close to his own. At first her body stiffened, and she tried to scratch him to make him let go.

She might as well have tried to make an automaton loosen its grip.

He felt no pity. It was not Lina who was before him. It was all of them. *Them*. Mankind.

Had they had any pity for him?

He went on gripping her throat, and her body went limp. Her legs gave way under her, and he had to hold her up.

Her mouth opened. Her pink tongue protruded between her lips, which little by little were losing their color. Her wide-open, bulging eyes still seemed to be asking:

"Why?"

And, if he had heard the question, he could only have replied:

"Because!"

He let her drop to the floor like a rag doll. His knees were shaking a little. He stared around the room, which was not his own. Did he even know exactly where he was?

He was not comfortable here. He crossed the landing to go back to his own apartment and had to let himself in with his key because Jeanne was not there.

He sat down in his armchair. He was tired. He did not ask himself questions. All that had happened was natural, inevitable; he had known that for years.

The dog tried to climb up his leg, and he bent down and lifted it onto his knees.

That was how Jeanne found the two of them. He was pleased to see her. He had waited for her for nearly two hours. It was good to have her with him again and to tell her the news.

"You know, I've killed her. . . ."

Épalinges
March 17, 1971